MEDUSA

SPEED DATING WITH THE DENIZENS OF THE UNDERWORLD

BOOK THIRTY

GINA KINCADE

NAUGHTY NIGHTS PRESS LLC• CANADA

MEDUSA

Fly away on the back of a green dragon? Yes, please!

Maddie Gordon is stuck in a bit of a rut. Work. Home. Wine. Sleep. Rinse and repeat. Providing daycare in the Underworld can be hellish fun, but she needs some adult time in her life.

When the perfect guy to jolt her out of the mundane cycle arrives in her life like a whirlwind, Maddie is literally swept off her feet. Unfortunately, all she got other than a pleasantly sore body was his first name... until he needs an alibi!

Dragon shifter Jaden McKellen is a fighter at Valhalla's Throne, and he's damn good at it. Forced to lose a fight, his brothers send him to the DeLux Café to blow off steam. Reluctant at first, he's grateful once he meets the gorgeous Maddie.

After a night of passion, Jaden returns home to find the police on his doorstep. Now his only alibi is a woman he thought he'd never see again.

Their chemistry is undeniable, so why does Jaden keep running away?

Medusa is book thirty in the Speed Dating with the Denizens of the Underworld shared world, featuring a tough-as-nails supernatural daycare provider, a broody dragon shifter, and more.

CHAPTER ONE

MEDUSA, KNOWN AS Maddie to her friends, woke up slowly one grey morning. The gloom outside made her want to curl up under her covers for another couple hours. She stretched languidly and glanced at her alarm clock. It was an old-fashioned kind, with red illuminated numbers.

The numbers were flashing 12:00.

"Shit!" Maddie cursed, grabbing at

her cell phone and almost dropping it in her haste to turn it on. "*Shit!*" she exclaimed again when she saw that it was almost eight in the morning. She whipped her covers off, scrambling gracelessly out of bed and stripping out of her tank top and short shorts that she wore to sleep. She didn't see where they'd landed, because she already had her t-shirt half on. She tucked her bra, underwear, and socks into a bag, yanked on a pair of comfy leggings, and half-ran, half-fell down the stairs.

She looked longingly at her coffee maker, but there was no time for that this morning. She grabbed a banana and granola bar, which joined her garments in the bag, and stepped into her running shoes before she was out the door.

The daycare she owned was only two

blocks away, thankfully, and she sprinted the short distance. She arrived out of breath and disheveled, just as the first parent was walking up the pathway.

"Hestia," she gasped at her assistant. "Do you mind..."

"Not a problem," Hestia reassured her calmly. "Hello Damien, are you excited to play with the dinosaurs again?"

The door closing behind her cut off the rest of the conversation. "First order of business, get properly dressed," Maddie said to herself, closing herself in her office. The clock on the wall told her she'd managed to make it from bed to work in less than five minutes. "Thank someone," she muttered and started fixing her clothing. She practically inhaled her breakfast before rejoining Hestia in the common space.

MEDUSA

Damien, age three, was playing with the large plastic dinosaurs they'd received yesterday. There was a Stegosaurus, a Triceratops, and of course, a Tyrannosaurus Rex. Damien had decided that the three-horned dinosaur was the baby and the other two were the parents.

Maddie deftly plucked the screw out of Shana's hands before it reached her mouth, the nine-month-old too young to understand the difference between food and toy. The baby screwed up her face, ready to scream, but then she spotted the dark haired Alexander and made happy babbles at him. The pretty toddler boy was only two, but he already had half the population of Purgatory wrapped around his little finger, and Maddie was no exception. Fortunately, he was a darling and the extra attention didn't do him any harm.

"Maddie," Hestia said in an undertone. "Lady Chloe is here to talk to you."

Maddie's eyebrows rose in surprise. Then she remembered that the Lord of the Underworld's wife worked above, in the human realm, and she'd gone back to her job recently after the birth of their first child six months ago. "I'll talk to her right away. Are you all right with them?" She indicated the kids happily playing on the floor.

"We'll be fine. Shoo," Hestia said gently, waving her hands in the direction of the kitchen. "And have some coffee."

"Yes, Mother," Maddie teased. In reality, she was desperate for the dark shot of caffeine and would probably do almost anything for some. "Hello, Lady Chloe," she greeted the blonde woman in her kitchen.

"Please, drop the honorific," Chloe pleaded. She had baby Atlanta in one arm and a to-go coffee from the ButterNut Bakery in her free hand. "I need to talk to you."

"I'm all ears," Maddie said, pulling down her favorite mug and pouring herself a cup from the coffee maker in the corner.

"Atlanta is..." Chloe trailed off, biting her lip.

Maddie waited patiently, the mug warming her hands as she cradled it.

"You know I'm a wolf shifter, right?" Chloe asked, turning the full force of her gaze on Maddie.

"Yes."

"And Lucifer's a demon."

"Naturally."

"Well... Atlanta's a little precocious." Chloe put the baby down on the ground gently.

The instant the baby's feet touched the tile, she transformed, her back legs becoming like those of a wolf. Tiny, ebony-colored, sparsely feathered wings sprouted from her shoulder blades. The rest of her stayed in human form, and she flopped around her mother's feet, crying piteously.

Chloe picked her up again and Atlanta turned full human once more. Chloe gestured at the baby, shrugging as if to say, "See?"

Maddie grinned. "That was incredible!" She directed her comments to the baby. "You're so good at that!"

"Not so great in a *human* daycare," Chloe said meaningfully. "Please, tell me you have room for her here? I don't know what else to do!"

"Of course we have room for her. I assume you wanted her close to your work so you could pop in and see her during the day," Maddie said.

"Exactly," Chloe interrupted. "But when *this* started happening…"

"I totally understand. Can you stick around this morning, let her get used to Hestia and I before you go during the afternoon?"

"Yes, yes, anything! My boss is fully aware that my hours will be shortened for the next while. They're very understanding, thankfully."

"Why don't we sit and talk?" Maddie suggested to Chloe. To the baby, she asked, "Atlanta, may I carry you to the couch?"

The baby hid her face in her mother's shoulder and Maddie nodded. "That's just fine. I'm a complete stranger to you."

Chloe chuckled. "Actually, she might be a little startled by your hair."

"My hair?" Maddie repeated, startled. "What..." She caught a glimpse of herself in the reflection cast by the window. "Yikes, that's quite the bedhead!" She immediately started running her fingers through the brilliant crimson strands, trying to calm it down. "There must have been a power surge or outage at my place last night. My alarm didn't go off this morning. I made it here with only seconds to spare!"

"Impressive," Chloe said.

After her hair was somewhat tamed, Maddie led the way to one of the squashy couches, grabbing a couple different sensory toys on the way, to help the baby get to know her.

She alternated conversations between mother and child. "You like the zebra?" Maddie asked the fascinated infant, who was now sitting comfortably on her mother's lap. "Would you like to hold it?"

The baby didn't make any movement to grab it, so Maddie made it prance across the distance between them and up Chloe's thigh. At the top, the zebra seemed to see the girl and shied away from her, hiding on the couch cushion.

"This is Atlanta. She's new here. It's okay to be a little scared of new things, Mister Zebra." Maddie deepened her voice to speak for the zebra, "I don't like new things! I only like you!" Back to her normal voice, she continued the one-sided conversation, "Aww, that's sweet. But I know you'll absolutely love Atlanta once you get to know her."

Atlanta leaned so far forward to see the stuffed animal that Chloe had to catch her before she fell off her mother's lap. "Ba!" the baby said, making grabby hands. "Bababa!"

"Zebra," Maddie enunciated clearly. "You would like the zebra?"

"Ba!" she shrieked delightedly when the zebra's head popped into her sight again, her wings reappearing on her back. She grabbed for the animal and Maddie surrendered the toy gracefully.

"I assume you would like to encourage her shifting?" Maddie said to Chloe while Atlanta was distracted with turning the animal around in her hands.

"Yes, of course." Chloe leaned back against the cushions and took a sip of her coffee. "Her wings are too fragile to carry her weight, as slight as she is, so we'll need to build up her muscles."

"As with any other muscle group at this age," Maddie agreed. "May I touch the wings?" she asked both of them.

Chloe nodded and Atlanta ignored her, so Maddie gently ran a finger over the top edge. "Similar to a baby bird with how the bones are arranged, soft down feathers, those will fluff out in time," Maddie muttered under her breath.

"You just had to mention the lack of feathers," Chloe put in, amused.

Maddie blushed. "Sorry. I assume they're similar to her father's?"

"Lucifer's are much bigger, but they

do seem to be built along the same lines," Chloe replied.

"How do you feel about her exploring on her own in the house and in the yard?" Maddie asked. "We can, of course, wear her if you'd prefer she not be let down..." she trailed off, letting Chloe talk.

"She does love to be held," Chloe said thoughtfully. "But I think letting her figure things out on her own would be good for her. It might encourage her to transform into a wolf the full way. You're fully fenced in, right?"

"Yes, and we keep a close eye on them at all times in case something dangerous made its way into the grounds and we missed it. What does she eat?"

"I'll give you a couple of bottles of

breastmilk every day, one for mid-morning, one for mid-afternoon. At lunch, she can have whatever the others are having, in bite-sized portions. She especially likes to feed herself cheese." Chloe smiled.

"Dairy isn't a problem, then?"

"No, no dietary restrictions that we've found so far. We've tested all the usual human and wolf intolerances, just to be safe."

"Smart," Maddie said. "Two naps?"

"Yes, one hour at ten and two hours at one-thirty, although if you wear her or she's feeling under the weather, she'll sleep longer."

"Naturally. Would you like to see the nap setup?" At Chloe's nod, Maddie reached out to Atlanta again. "May I hold you?"

The baby launched herself gleefully into her arms, making Maddie laugh and smile down at the child. "I like you, too."

She led Chloe to a room beyond the kitchen that had several portable cribs set up. "We can move them around, depending on the child. Some prefer to sleep in a noisy environment, so we would bring the crib into the main room for them. On hot days, we pull them outside and set up sun shades in the breezeway."

"That's fantastic," Chloe said enthusiastically. "Should we bring anything from home for her?"

"Anything you think might make her feel more comfortable. For children as young as Atlanta, we generally suggest a t-shirt that you've worn recently, so that they can smell something comforting that reminds them of home. Breastmilk, of course. Diapers, if she has sensitive skin. We don't put any diaper cream, unless she's having troubles, because it's better for their skin to breathe. When were you thinking of potty training her?" Maddie kept her expression neutral.

Chloe laughed. "We haven't even considered potty training yet! When she shows interest in it, I guess."

"That's a good attitude to have. Every child reacts differently to potty training, and you don't want to push her into something before she's ready for it. We will follow your lead on potty training when it's time, so that she doesn't get mixed messages." Maddie led them back into the playroom.

Atlanta froze when she saw the other children, the zebra dangling by one leg from her mouth.

Maddie chuckled. "Would you like to play with them?" She sat cross-legged on the ground and put Atlanta in the relative safety of her lap. "This is Shana, Alexander, and Damien." She pointed at each child in turn, who mostly didn't look up from what they were doing.

Encouraged by their disinterest in a new playmate, Atlanta reached out for a nearby block and swapped the zebra for it, drool running down her chin.

"Teething, are you?" Maddie said. "We'll get you a frozen teether and put it with Lyta's. She can commiserate with you, poor thing."

"Her fifth," Chloe supplied, sitting beside them.

"And you're still nursing her? Brave woman," Maddie said.

Chloe laughed ruefully. "She learned *very* quickly not to bite me or she'd lose access to her food."

"That would do it," Maddie said, smiling in sympathy.

"I'm so glad you had space for her," Chloe said, reaching out and squeezing Maddie's hand. "Human-wolf babies with wings are rather frowned upon in Earth daycares."

Maddie almost choked on her laughter. "You think?"

CHAPTER TWO

"FOR *FUCK'S* SAKE, get your head out of your ass and get laid already!" Augustine roared, two inches from Jaden's face.

Jaden was impressed. Augustine had actually used the slang correctly for once. "Maybe you're the one who should get laid!" he shouted back, wiping spittle from his face. "You're so testy, you're obviously not getting any!" He loved goading his big brother about his sex life, not that Augustine was ever forthcoming with details, despite being mated to the Goddess Hera.

"My temper has nothing to do with how much sex I've had lately and *everything* to do with you waking me up at the crack of dawn every morning this week by tackling me out of bed!" Augustine growled. "Maybe if I got a full night of sleep, I would find you more *tolerable!*"

"Tolerable?" Jaden sputtered. "Forgive me for wanting to spend more *time* with my brothers!"

"As if! You wake me up, drag me outside for a run, and then take off. We never spend *time* together!"

"Maybe if you weren't such an *old man* and *slow as fuck* you'd be able to keep up with me!" Jaden shouted back.

"I'm only four years older than you, and if I'm slow, it's because I have not had enough sleep!" Augustine pointed at the doorway. "Out! Now, before I throw you out on your ass! And stay the fuck out of my room!"

"You can't kick me out of my own house!" Jaden growled. "I pay my equal share."

Augustine snarled, his purple dragon scales rippling over the skin of his face, half-transforming between one breath and the next.

Shit.

All right, here we go.

Jaden twitched, feeling his dragon starting to make its appearance.

But Augustine had more control over his form, and as he caught an untransformed Jaden up in his powerful jaws, Jaden had to concentrate on hardening the skin around his abdomen where Augustine's teeth were uncomfortably close to tender organs.

Augustine spat him out the front door, Jaden rolling head over heels on the hard flagstone path until he came to a stop flat on his back by the front gate.

"Come back when you are in a better frame of mind," Augustine growled, snorting smoke out of his nostrils. "Whatever that might take." He slammed the door closed behind him.

Jaden flipped the bird at the house and rubbed the back of his head. "Fuck," he said quietly, feeling a knot forming. He sat up slowly, the house across the street swaying in his vision until he blinked a couple times and his dragon healing kicked in. Using the gate, he struggled to his feet and brushed dirt from the path off his clothes. Fortunately, there were no rips in his shirt or jeans, and the dirt fell to the ground with little persuasion.

"This wouldn't have happened if Finley were home," Jaden said, sulking as he started down their street to the main part of Purgatory. "He would have stopped *Auggie* from throwing me out." He spat the name of his brother along with a wad of saliva onto the side of the road. It was tinged with blood and he scowled at it.

"'Just go pick up a woman,'" he said, imitating his brother's voice. "'What, like it's hard?' Bah!"

Once he reached the main street, Jaden paused, considering his options. He could go to Valhalla's Throne, but he'd already fought there today, and he'd lost. Badly. He didn't want to risk running into Pollux again after the words they'd shared earlier that evening.

Jaden groaned. "I wish I could redo this whole day," he lamented. "Somewhere with alcohol, then. Drink to forget, right?"

A flash of shimmery purple material caught his eye, and he watched a striking blonde walk into the Underworld Cafe. "Now *that's* what I'm talking about," he muttered under his breath. He crossed the street, paused to fix his hair in his reflection in the cafe's windows, and opened the door.

Please, let one thing go right for me today.

***

The day had started as usual. Jaden woke early, downed a protein shake, stretched in preparation for his run, woke his brothers, and then headed out for his run.

What would they do without me?

Waste the whole day sleeping?

He chuckled at the thought. He ran in silence, enjoying the cool morning air as he worked up a sweat.

Once back at the house, he spent some time with the weights in the backyard, two-hundred-pound weights in each hand. His brothers had left to do their own thing by the time he'd entered the house, and he took his time in the shower. Then a high protein, high carb lunch, because his fight was scheduled for the dinner rush and he wouldn't eat much beforehand.

MEDUSA

Odin requested that his fighters arrive at least an hour before their scheduled appearances, so Jaden made his way to the brothers' ready room with time to spare. He wanted to get in a few leg reps in the fight club's workout space. It was the one thing they didn't have at home; a good machine to work out the legs.

Jaden laid out his fight uniform on the chair in his room, a pair of loose black shorts with green scales on the sides, and returned to the hallway.

"Watch it," growled a deep voice, pushing past him as he closed his door.

"Watch it yourself," Jaden snarked back. "Am I not visible enough for you?" He faced off against one of the biggest bullies in Valhalla's Throne.

Most of the fighters employed by Odin

were the amicable sort; willing to play up a character in the ring, not holding any grudges once out. Pollux, the brute he was going toe-to-toe with right now, was *not* that sort.

Fuck, am I ever looking forward to mopping the floor with him tonight, Jaden let his smug amusement show on his face as he stared Pollux down.

"Hey, keep it in the ring, boys." One of the members of Odin's security team put his arm between the fighters.

Pollux sneered. "You need these weak-ass boys to do the fighting for you, J-Star? Too chicken to fight me without the precious rules of the ring?"

Jaden took a deep breath, trying to cool his quick temper. "I'm not going to get kicked out of the club because I was picking fights outside the ring. You want your fight? Come and get it at six tonight."

"Rules," Pollux spat. He pushed the security guy's arm away from him. "I don't need you!" He pretended to take a jab at Jaden, who didn't flinch, making Pollux even angrier. The demigod stormed off down the hallway, on the way to the ring to watch the fights before his own.

"You okay?"

Jaden rolled his head on his neck, getting rid of some of the tension that had crept in. "Fine, thanks." He hated that every nerve now felt on edge. Hopefully a good workout would get his head in the right mindset for the fight tonight.

He groaned internally. He'd yet to roll the dice to see whether he'd win or lose tonight.

The dragon shifter brothers had decided together, when they'd started fighting in Odin's underground fighting club, that they would roll a dice before each match to see whether they would win or lose. Without that random chance, there was no way they would ever lose, and that just wasn't interesting for the spectators. Nobody knew that they decided the outcome of the match beforehand, and they wanted to keep it that way.

Nobody'll know if I just...

Don't roll the dice tonight.

Jaden pondered as he huffed and puffed away at the leg press, the weights set to only three hundred pounds. He was planning on doing a high rep to make up for the low weight.

Ugh.

I would know.

And I would feel guilty if I didn't roll.

But what if I roll a one?

He left the leg press and moved on to the squat rack, his mind still on his ethical conundrum.

If I don't roll tonight, why would I ever bother to roll again?

That's not fair to Augustine or Finley.

After his workout, Jaden headed back to the ready room, intent on a shower and a quick protein bar before his match with Pollux.

The bright blue die in the bottom of his bag mocked him as he pulled his towel out. Without thinking about it any further, he scooped it up and rolled it on the table.

A one.

Fuck.

A cold shower was just what the doctor ordered after that. Jaden rubbed down quickly with soap, his skin rippling with goosebumps under the frigid water. He dried off just as quickly, trying to figure out how to go about this fight. Pollux had a strong arm, but he tended to overreach with his left. If Jaden had been allowed to win, he would take advantage of that, but now he knew he had to keep the fight close, with lots of grappling. Not that he particularly minded grappling. It was his preferred method of fighting, a lot like a bar brawl. But it meant that he'd probably get pretty hurt, maybe even a concussion. Jaden was grateful for his quick healing, so something like that wouldn't be a problem after a few minutes.

He grinned. Just because he had to lose, didn't mean he couldn't rough Pollux up a bit first. The demigod could take a hit. Jaden grudgingly gave him that.

He put on an athletic cup and yanked his shorts on overtop. He grabbed a sweat towel and draped it over his shoulders, and then he was ready.

"Let's get this over with," Jaden muttered to himself.

When he got backstage, he saw that there were fifteen minutes left on the clock for the fight ahead of him. He felt limber, after his workout, but still went through the motions of the necessary stretches. Even though he could heal quickly, a torn muscle would still hurt like a bitch.

"Hey Princess, are you ready to lose?" Pollux greeted him, putting his foot on Jaden's back while he was stretching in the splits.

The sudden added pressure made his groin muscles spasm and he sucked in an involuntary breath.

"Get away from him." Another of Odin's security, a woman this time, stepped in, and Pollux backed off.

"Hey, if he can't take the heat, maybe he should get out of the oven," Pollux sneered.

Jaden slowly shook out his muscles. The added stretch hadn't hurt him, thankfully. "If you can't fight fair, maybe you shouldn't be here at all," he said evenly.

"Aww, are widdle Pwincess's feewings hurt?" Pollux said in a baby voice. "Face me like a man, J-Star."

The bell signaled the end of the previous fight, and the volume of the applause increased, even backstage. The two fighters, dripping sweat and blood, walked slowly through on their way to their ready rooms, arms slung around each other in support.

Jaden looked after them longingly. He wouldn't get that tonight. He refocused on Pollux. "Well, that's where you're wrong. I'm no human."

Pollux snorted. "Even if you were, you won't be after I'm through with you."

"That makes no sense," Jaden grumbled, bouncing a little on his toes as they stood, waiting to be called into the ring.

"I'm going to rip off your manhood and feed it to you," Pollux hissed.

"Dramatic, much," Jaden replied mildly. "Maybe *you're* the princess."

He was saved from Pollux's reply by his name being called by the announcer.

"Please welcome to the ring, Jaden "J-Star" McKellen! Top heavyweight in his class!" the announcer's voice rang through the amphitheatre.

Jaden entered the ring with his arms in the air to cheers from the crowd. He smiled and blew a couple kisses, shaking a couple hands from the front row, before joining the announcer on the far side of the ring.

"Tonight, J-Star is up against Pollux "Demigod" Begrond. Pollux has been in this class for a while, but hasn't managed to make it up the rankings, always knocked down by one or another of the brothers. Put your hands together for Pollux!"

Jaden was pleased to note that the enthusiasm was slightly less for his opponent.

Pollux didn't work up the crowd the way he had, and the fight started quickly.

Jaden led Pollux in a slow dance across the sands, drawing out his left until he was off balance. Jaden saw his chance and tackled Pollux down to the ground, straddling his torso and raining down blows around Pollux's head. The demigod had to keep his hands up around his ears to protect himself, but his legs were free.

Jaden saw the hip flip coming from a mile away and sighed internally. He had to make this look like Pollux had won fairly, after all. He resisted the first hip toss, but pretended like it knocked him enough off balance that the second threw him on his side. Pollux followed up on his apparent advantage, hooking his leg around Jaden's to pin him to the ground.

He'll never learn if I don't keep him on his toes.

Jaden executed a twist and backward somersault that had him free in seconds. Pollux was still on the ground on his knees, looking shocked.

"Right where you belong," Jaden said boisterously, making the audience laugh. He fisted a hand in Pollux's hair and thrust his hips provocatively.

The demigod snarled, grabbing Jaden's wrist and pulling himself up with it.

"I'd be happy to lend you a hand

anytime you need it," Jaden quipped, provoking more laughter. "The way you act, you probably need some stress relief sooner rather than later." He caught a hard punch on his abdomen from Pollux's right, and staggered a bit, bending over. Pollux followed it up with a blow from his knee to Jaden's forehead.

The fight devolved from there.

***

Finley found Jaden sitting on the floor of the shower, leaning against the cool tiles in an effort to stop his head from pounding.

"You just *had* to provoke him, didn't you?" Finley said.

"Shhhhh," Jaden murmured. "I had to make it look good, didn't I?"

Finley rolled his eyes. "He knock you silly? You didn't have to lose by this much."

"It'll make my comeback even sweeter," Jaden said. "He still out there bragging?"

"Of course he is." Finley scoffed. "And he'll stay out there until you come out of here because he wants to humiliate you. Did you really say it?"

"I said a lot of things. Could you be more specific?" Jaden mumbled. Of course he knew what Finley was really asking about.

"Did you threaten to kill him?"

"He punched me in the cup, Finn." Jaden flexed bruised knuckles. "I was pissed."

"Yeah, well, I guess someone had to take that hit."

MEDUSA

"Fuck you."

***

A change into his dragon had healed the worst of the aches and pains; there was still a nice purple bruise on his side. Jaden examined his eye closely in the reflection of the cafe window. Fortunately, the bruising there wouldn't show up until tomorrow morning, he knew from experience.

Satisfied with his appearance, he opened the door, hearing the cheerful ringing of the bells over his head.

"Oh, perfect! Fresh meat!" said a sultry voice.

"What?" Jaden was pulled further into the cafe by long fingers with even longer red nails. "Oh no."

CHAPTER THREE

"RAWR!" DAMIEN ROARED in Maddie's ear, making her head pound.

"Are you a dinosaur?" she asked, staving off further shouts.

"I'm a Damiosaur!" the three-year-old declared proudly.

"Wow! And what does a Damiosaur eat?" Maddie asked.

Gosh, her charges were cute.

Damien thought about that. "He eats

mac and cheese!"

"What a coincidence! That's what we're having for lunch today!" Maddie checked on Alexander and Atlanta, who were investigating the contents of the toy box, and Hestia, who was changing Lyta's diaper. "Would you like to help me *make* it?"

"Yes, please!" Damien said with a huge grin.

"Excellent. Can you put away the dinosaurs and wait for me at the kitchen door?" Receiving an affirmative nod from the child, Maddie moved toward the toy box excavators. "It's going to be lunchtime in about twenty minutes, okay? Alexander, do you think you can show Atlanta how to put toys in the box?"

Alexander sighed. "At'ta know how."

"She's still very little. She needs to be reminded. Atlanta, new game!" Maddie injected excitement into her voice as she picked up a stuffed toy. "Can you help the bunny walk into her home?" She gave the bunny to the baby, who giggled and made it bounce in front of her. "That's right, hop the bunny into the toy box!" Maddie pointed, enforcing the concept.

Atlanta pulled herself to standing, using the side of the box for support, and hopped the bunny through the air until it reached the box, dropping it in with a flourish.

"Oh, great job sweetie! Do you see any other toys that belong in this home?" Maddie asked. She nudged Alexander with the back of her hand and he picked up a rattle, giving it to the baby, who stuck it in her mouth. "Where does the rattle go? Can you put it away?" Maddie prompted.

Atlanta took a moment to think that concept over and then dropped the rattle on top of the bunny.

"Yes!" Maddie encouraged Alexander to continue the game. "Remember to use your words, honey. Get excited for her when she does it, encourage her when she's struggling. Hestia is here to help you, okay?"

"'Kay."

"You're such a great help. Thank you so much, Alexander." Maddie beamed at him, which made him smile back before turning his attention to his job.

The two women exchanged nods and Maddie headed for the kitchen. Damien was waiting for her beside the gated room, drawing on the chalkboard wall with green chalk. "You may open the gate now. Thank you for your patience."

"What are we putting in it?" Damien asked, popping the locking mechanism and struggling with the enclosure.

"We have zucchini, mushrooms, and bacon in the fridge," Maddie said. "I can fry that up while the noodles are boiling. What do you think?"

"Can I use the knife?" Damien asked, eyes shining.

Maddie laughed. "Only with supervision."

"I know," Damien said with a heavy sigh.

"But first, we need to make the pasta. Can you get the pot and the frying pan after you wash your hands with me, please?"

"Yes!"

With Damien's help, Maddie had the water on the stovetop and the bacon sizzling in the frying pan in no time. She'd cut the bacon into baby-bite size before cooking it and then guided Damien's hand while he carefully cut the zucchini sticks into small pieces.

"Are you going to help me pour the noodles into the pot?" She watched as he climbed onto the step stool beside the stove and slowly poured the noodles into the now boiling water.

"Do you mind if I finish up the zucchini, or do you want me to help you with the last bits?"

"Help me!"

Heaving an internal sigh, Maddie waited until he'd put the stool back at the cutting board and climbed up. Once everything was cut, Damien poured the zucchini into the bacon grease still in the frying pan to cook.

"What now?" he asked happily.

"Now we need the table set. Lyta sometimes uses the baby fork, so put one of those at her place, please. Small forks for you and Alexander, big ones for Hestia and I. I'll pour water in the glasses and you can bring them out *one at a time!*" she emphasized. Last week, he'd tried to take two and ended up looking half-drowned. At least it was just water. His clothes had dried by the time his mom had arrived to pick him up at the end of the day.

She grated the cheese and cut the mushrooms while he made several trips to the table with all the utensils and glasses, moving the zucchini around once in a while to cook it evenly.

"Five minute warning," Maddie called into the other room after testing a noodle and finding it the perfect softness. "Alexander, what does that mean for you?"

"Pee on potty," the two-year-old called back.

"Very good. Don't forget to make a checkmark on your reward sheet after you wash your hands."

Damien returned to the kitchen, hands empty.

"What about you, mister? Can you think about your body?"

"I don't have to pee," he insisted.

"Are you sure? You've had to leave the table twice this week already," Maddie reminded him.

Damien sighed, his shoulders

sagging. "I guess."

"Good boy."

At the end of the day, Hestia was cleaning up the kitchen while Maddie played with Atlanta on the floor.

"Come on, At'ta, you want the toy. I know you want the car. Come and get it."

The little girl burbled cheerfully and flapped her wings slightly, the claws of her hind legs scratching on the vinyl flooring.

"Oh no! Atlanta!"

Maddie swiveled around to greet the newcomer. "Don't worry about it, Chloe. These floors can take a little beating. She's doing so well."

"Is she?" Chloe sat beside her on the floor. "I've only really seen the babies from my pack. And Heidi's, of course."

She was talking about her best friend, who'd had twins a little over a year ago.

"How are those babies different from Atlanta?" Maddie asked, rolling the car back and forth to keep the baby's attention.

"They're older when they first transform, so they're usually walking already. Their first transformation is a little rough, but it's complete, and they can walk around after the first few tumbles." Chloe leaned over and grabbed a soft doll. She made it wave at the baby, who gurgled.

"Fascinating. She's advanced in some ways, but not in others," Maddie said thoughtfully. "I'm trying to encourage her to either crawl or transform fully, depending on her preference. Mobility is good for her. It'll help build her muscles.

Atlanta rocked back and forth on her hands and clawed feet again, flapping her wings for balance. She let out a shriek of impatience.

"Yes, sweetheart, I know you can do it. One hand at a time," Maddie encouraged. She glanced at the clock. "Okay, it's been about five minutes now. I think it's time to rest. We'll try again tomorrow."

Chloe bum scooted forward and picked up the little girl, who turned fully human once in her mother's arms. "Were you a good girl today, my darling?"

The baby happily patted her mother's face and then tugged on the neckline of her shirt, nuzzling into her breast.

"Do you mind if I nurse her here?" Chloe asked.

"Not at all! Make yourself comfortable." Maddie gestured at the couch. "I'm just going to tidy up a bit and pass the mop over the floors. It won't distract her?"

"From the way she's rooting, I don't think a tornado would distract her!" Chloe said with a chuckle, hiking up the hem of her shirt and unclasping the cup of her bra.

Maddie scooped up the toys that hadn't quite made it to the toy box. The kids were pretty good about cleaning up after themselves, for the most part. It was one of the things that parents constantly thanked them for; teaching the children how to tidy up after themselves, even for children as young as Atlanta.

It was a lot of work, but so worth it.

Maddie scanned the playroom for more toys, only holding a handful. Toys deposited in their boxes, she turned her attention to mopping, only picking up some drool patches and a little bit of sand near the back door when they'd entered after playing outside that afternoon.

Hestia waved her off with a soapy hand, snagging the mop from her hands, so Maddie left her be and let herself relax next to Chloe, who was fending off Atlanta's hand as it waved in her face.

"I think she missed you," Maddie said mischievously.

"I missed her, too," Chloe said fervently. "It's only eight hours or so, but seeing her again at the end of the day is so great. I really appreciate every minute I get to spend with her, you know?"

Maddie nodded. "I know what you mean. At least your commute isn't too bad, right?"

Chloe chuckled. "One of the benefits of having the Lord of the Underworld as your husband; he's very well connected." She cocked her head at Maddie. "Speaking of which, I heard you tried speed dating about a year ago, but then never went back."

"Ugh, don't remind me!" Maddie groaned. "What a disaster *that* was!"

"The men in Purgatory are idiots if they don't want you," Chloe said, eyebrows rising in surprise.

"Them wanting me wasn't the problem," Maddie confided with a shake of her head. "The problem was that they didn't want *me.*"

"Sorry, I don't follow."

"They wanted a sex doll."

"Oh." Chloe rolled her eyes. "Then they're doubly idiots. You need a guy who will like you for you, not just your body."

"And I'm not sure I'll find that at speed dating." Maddie wrinkled her nose.

"I did." Chloe nodded, smiling at Maddie's shocked expression. "Didn't you know that? Demi and Hera both found their true loves there as well. Ouch, Atlanta, no teeth!"

Maddie thought about what Chloe had said while the mother fussed over her baby. "I don't know..."

"Someone very smart told my daughter not long ago that 'it's okay to be scared of new things.' Maybe you should take her advice." Chloe smirked.

"You just aren't playing fair," Maddie said with a pout. "Throwing my own words back at me."

"They were wise words. Wear something similar to what you've got on now." Chloe gestured at Maddie. "You're not showing off your body, but you still look cute."

"This?" Maddie glanced down at her simple t-shirt and jeans. She nodded. "Yeah, that could work," she said slowly.

"Be open to the unexpected. You never know what might happen," Chloe said. She winked. "The next speed dating event is tonight. You got this, girl!"

"Tonight," Maddie gasped. "Oh man."

***

While getting dressed after her shower, Maddie had second thoughts about dressing so casually. She remembered how the women had dressed to the nines at the last event she'd been to, making her feel dowdy even though she'd been wearing her best dress. "If I dress even more casually, will I stick out even more?" she worried aloud, staring at her reflection in the mirror. Her gaze slid critically over her body, bare in preparation for whatever clothing she would decide to put on. Her breasts were on the small side, her ribs protruded too much to be attractive, and her belly was soft. Her hips were wide, but she felt like her ass was too flat. Her gaze snapped back up to her face, heart-shaped and surrounded by the riot of red curls that looked as if they moved on their own. Maddie sighed and picked up her brush, attempting to tame them.

MEDUSA

Her mother had told her that she was descended from the original Medusa, the turn-to-stone-if-you-looked-at-her Medusa. Maddie, fortunately, was spared that curse. She could, if she needed to defend herself, sing a high note and use that to target her enemy and turn them to stone, albeit only temporarily. She'd only needed to use it twice in her life, both times when a man didn't understand that no actually meant no.

Maddie gathered her hair up into a high ponytail and then pulled out a cute circle skirt that she hadn't yet had a chance to wear. It was a light grey with green polka dots, so she grabbed a v-neck t-shirt that matched the green and pulled that on over a simple bra. She had to change her underwear, because the material of the skirt clung in all the wrong places and she could see panty lines. "Thong it is," she muttered. "Whatever."

The walk over to the DeLux Cafe was nice, the air was warm, but there was a breeze to keep her cool. Her feet didn't hurt because she'd decided that her usual running shoes were probably the best choice. It's not like the men would notice her feet; they'd be sitting down most of the time anyway.

"Welcome back, Maddie!" Eve, the blonde vampire, greeted her with a large grin. "We've missed you."

"Uh, thank you?" Maddie wasn't sure how to respond to the enthusiasm. "I'm hoping tonight will go better than last time."

Eve frowned. "Me too. Sorry about

that. We do try to arrange matches for everyone, but some people are trickier than others."

"I don't mind being tricky," Maddie said with a chuckle.

"That is a wonderful attitude to have." Aphrodite, the dark-haired literal Goddess inserted herself into the conversation. "Don't you look sweet tonight, Maddie, dear. The men won't be able to keep their eyes off of you."

"That's not really the effect I was going for," Maddie said.

"Then you shouldn't be so beautiful," Aphrodite said as if it was the easiest compliment in the world. "Have you signed in yet?"

"No, just getting to that." Maddie picked up the clipboard Eve pushed toward her and moved aside to make room when a vision in a purple shimmery dress entered the cafe. In the back of her consciousness, she heard the two speed dating organizers greet the newcomer by name, but she didn't fully pay attention to anything beyond the form she filled out.

After she returned everything to Eve, Aphrodite took her by the arm and led her into the main room, which seemed to be full of people. "If you don't mind finding a seat, we'll get started shortly."

"Thank you," Maddie said.

The woman in purple entered and chose a seat on the left, closest to the door. She wanted to put as much distance between herself and the fancily dressed women in the room as possible, but there didn't seem to be anyone else dressed like her that she could sit near.

Sighing in resignation, because she was again starting to regret her decisions that had led her to being here, dressed like this, she chose a seat as close to the bar and kitchen door as possible. She hoped to signal someone who worked there that she needed a drink. A stiff one.

But Aphrodite hopped up onto the little stage. "You have five minutes to date your partner before the men switch tables. You'll be given ten seconds to mark down your compatibility on your ballots before you start your new date. Any questions?" Aphrodite paused, looking around the room for raised hands. "Find your seats and you may begin!" She rang a little bell on a tall table next to her.

There was a flurry of movement as

everyone hurried to take a seat.

CHAPTER FOUR

JADEN, PINNED BY the vampire's eager expression, filled out the form for speed dating.

Ugh, really?

How do I get myself into these situations?

He could hear another woman speaking into a microphone in the other room, telling the other people the rules of the event. He rolled his eyes, keeping his head down so that Eve wouldn't be offended.

It wasn't a good idea to have a vampire mad at you, after all.

Once he'd finished, Eve took his arm, her pointed, long, red fingernails digging into his bicep, and steered him into the main room of the cafe. Jaden got an overwhelming impression of *people*, and then he was being pushed into the empty seat in front of the woman in the shimmery purple dress.

"You may begin!" Aphrodite finished her speech and rang a bell.

Jaden flashed a winning smile at the blonde woman seated across from him. "Hi, I'm Jaden."

"Pandora," she replied.

"You look absolutely stunning today, Pandora," Jaden said.

"Oh, thanks."

Pandora seemed put off by his compliment, for some reason. Jaden spent the rest of the mini date trying to get her to show some sort of emotion, but came up dry.

Ugh, if all these dates are going to be this draining, maybe I should give up now, try to pull someone at Athens Bar a few blocks over instead.

Jaden moved to the next table, sliding into the chair across from a dark-haired, sultry-eyed woman.

"Good evening, handsome. I'm Dakota, what's your name?" the flashy brunette asked, leaning so far forward that Jaden could see down her cleavage.

All right, this is better.

Jaden grinned at the thought.

But as the conversation wore on,

Dakota turning everything he said into a sexual innuendo, Jaden started to tire of her.

I need someone sexy, but not overtly so.

Someone interesting and interested.

Does a girl like that even exist?

Four more dates, each with something about them that didn't quite do it for him. Jaden was starting to think this whole evening was going to be a wash, when he reached a table in the farthest corner of the room, near the kitchen. The redhead seated there wore a simple t-shirt in a vibrant green that matched his scales perfectly. She smiled at him and leaned forward, saying, "Do you happen to know how I could possibly get some food? I didn't get a chance to eat dinner and I'm starving."

Jaden chuckled. "I think you'll have to wait until the dates are over."

The woman glanced over his shoulder and groaned. "I don't have the patience to wait that long. This whole evening has been, in a word, abysmal."

"I was thinking the same thing." Jaden cocked an eyebrow up at her. "What would you say to skipping out on the rest of it? I know an awesome little bakery that's still open for the next half hour."

The woman bit her plush bottom lip, her gaze darting around the room. "I don't know..."

"Come on. When was the last time you did something fun, just for yourself?"

She grinned and flipped her ponytail over her shoulder, her blue eyes sparkling with mischief. "Too long. How are we going to sneak out of here?"

Jaden suppressed a chuckle. He'd been planning on getting up and walking out the front door, but if she wanted to play James Bond, who was he to deny her? "The kitchens. When it's time to change tables, I'll cause a distraction and we'll slip out the back door."

"Okay! Glad I wore my running shoes."

She was too cute. Satisfied with his choice, Jaden watched Aphrodite out of the corner of his eye. "Get ready," he murmured as the Goddess walked over to the bell.

The woman across from him shifted, sliding her knees out from under the table.

The bell rang and all the men got to

their feet. In the chaos of chairs scraping across the floor, Jaden's tail flicked out and knocked into the man on his left, causing him to spill his wine across the table and into the lap of the woman still sitting there.

She let out a shriek of dismay and leapt to her feet, red wine staining the front of her dress.

"I'll get you some napkins," Jaden said immediately, jumping to his feet and heading for the bar. He grabbed a handful and thrust them into the hands of the man he'd tripped. "You can thank me later," he whispered with a wink.

A bunch of people had converged on the unfortunate pair, all shouting different ways of getting stains out of clothing.

Jaden grasped the mystery woman's

hand and pulled her through the kitchen door, peeking back out through the window to see if anyone had noticed them. "Coast is clear. We're good to go," he said in an undertone.

The woman giggled. "My hero."

"I'm not a hero," Jaden scoffed. "Let's get out of here."

The chefs in the kitchen barely gave them a passing glance as they made their way to the back door.

One of the benefits of not dressing up, Jaden thought, watching the skirt swish around the legs of the woman in front of him. It clung to her ass in all the right places, making his mouth water in appreciation.

"ButterNut Bakery is this way," Jaden said once they were outside.

"Oh, I love their food," she exclaimed

happily. "Great idea. My name's Maddie, by the way."

"Jaden."

"Nice to meet you."

"It's been an adventure so far," Jaden replied with a grin.

They were served quickly and chose to eat at a nearby park, because the bakery was closing soon.

Maddie bit into her sub sandwich and groaned in enjoyment. "Oh my gosh, I needed that."

Picking at his soft pretzel, Jaden smirked at her obvious pleasure. "Never skip meals."

"No kidding," she said around her bite, covering her mouth with one hand. "So, tell me about you."

"I'm not very interesting," Jaden drawled. "I mostly spend my days working out and working. I live with my brothers. What about you? What do you do?"

"I run a daycare center. I read a lot, garden a bit, and that's pretty much it." She blushed. "Sorry I'm not more interesting."

"That's a silly thing to apologize for," Jaden said with a frown. "I think you're fascinating. Tell me about the daycare."

Maddie launched into a story about her charges, and Jaden was surprised to find himself actually listening. She was so animated when talking about her work, it was obvious she loved doing it.

"Sorry," she said after a few minutes of non-stop chatter. "I could go on and on about the kids. They're so awesome."

"They sound awesome," Jaden agreed with a smile. "Stop apologizing." He leaned over and wiped a spot of mayo from the corner of her mouth with his thumb, and she froze, eyes wide. "You okay?"

"Yeah, I just... Wasn't expecting you to..." she stumbled over her words, obviously shy.

"Touch you?" Jaden asked, lowering his voice. "I couldn't resist. I've been dying to get my hands on you since the moment I saw you."

"Oh!" If anything, she blushed even more. "Really?"

"Darling, if you weren't eating that sandwich, I'd have pulled you into my lap to kiss you the instant we sat down," Jaden said boldly, since she seemed to be responding well to his advances.

She looked down at the sub in her hands as if she'd forgotten it was there, and then around at the playground. There were a couple families still present, and she bit her lip. "You know, my house is just around the corner…" she trailed off.

Jaden grinned down at her. "Miss Maddie, are you inviting me into your bed?"

"If we make it that far," she replied coyly, tossing her ponytail.

"I think you and I are going to get along just fine," Jaden said, standing and holding his hand out for her. "You can eat on the way."

"Good, because I really am starving."

"Can't have you fainting from hunger in the middle of the best pleasure you've ever received," Jaden said.

"Is that a promise?"

"You bet it is, baby."

Maddie finished her sandwich and they both quickened their pace. She led him up the front walk of a small two-storey house with pretty flowers out front.

"Nice place," he said, and meant it.

"Thank you. But I didn't bring you here to admire my exterior landscaping abilities."

Jaden almost choked on his laughter. "By all means, lead the way." He gestured at the front door with a slight bow. She put the key in the lock, and he pressed his body against her back, nuzzling behind her ear. "You smell so sweet," he murmured.

Her body shook a little, her fingers not moving to turn the key in the lock, her breathing shallow.

He brought his hands up to her

waist, slipping under her shirt and around to the front. He pressed slow kisses against the thin skin behind her ear and down the column of her neck, tracing the softness of her abdomen up to her ribs. "Is this okay?" he asked, nervous by her lack of verbal response.

Maddie nodded vigorously, her free hand coming up to brace herself against the opaque window of the front door.

Encouraged that she did actually want this, he moved faster now, both hands coming up to cup her breasts through her bra, and biting lightly at the meat where her shoulder met her neck, where his dragon urged he could place his mating bite.

Not now, damn it, he growled at his beast.

Knees buckling, Maddie collapsed

against him with a gasp.

"Open the door, darling. I need to get you naked, whether we're in public or not," Jaden growled.

Her fingers fumbled with the key even as he undid the front clasp of her bra and plucked at her nipples. Finally, she got it open and they stumbled inside, Jaden kicking the door closed behind him with one foot. He kept her pulled tight against him and walked her to the wall, pressing her against it, sliding one thigh between hers to keep her legs apart. "I want you to grind your pretty little pussy on my thigh when I do something you like, all right?"

"Yes," Maddie said, breathing heavily.

Jaden was delighted that she was playing along. His lips ghosted over the exposed skin on the back of her neck while he played with her breasts, pinching and twisting the nipples between his thumb and forefinger. Her hips rocked over his jean-clad thigh, her heat tangible even through the thick material. When her nipples were drawn in tight pearls, he switched tactics. "I've been dying to know what you've got on under this skirt..." He started pulling it up inch by inch. "Because it shows off your ass to perfection."

"It's nothing exci—" she started.

"Hush. I'll decide if it's exciting or not." His hands reached the end of the skirt. "Hold this for me, won't you?" He flipped the skirt up, putting it into her hands where they rested against the wall. "I want to explore."

"Okay," she said shakily.

"You're so gorgeous," he murmured,

gliding his hands over her bare thighs. His explorations didn't meet any material until right in the middle. "Who gave you the right to be so sexy." He growled low in his throat. His dragon answered the growl with a purr of its own.

She chuckled a little nervously. "It was the only option I had."

"Stay put. I need to look at you." Jaden took a step back and groaned, pressing the heel of his hand to his confined dick. "Fuck, look at you, spread out like a buffet for me." He covered her body with his again, making sure she could feel just how affected he was by her. "I've got a million and one ideas on how to play this. Do you have any fantasies that you want me to fulfill?"

"I... I don't know," she said

breathlessly. "I'm liking this... Being ordered around and put on display."

Jaden grinned. "Oh yes, we are going to have so much fun tonight." In a quick movement, he spun her around and scooped her up, pressing her back against the wall. "Lift your shirt. Show me those breasts," he ordered.

Blushing slightly, she lifted the green material up to her shoulders, the cups of her bra swinging loose.

"Beautiful," Jaden complimented both her body and her actions. "Arms out."

Her shirt immediately dropped when she did what he asked.

"Up," he demanded.

It took her a minute to understand what he was getting at, and then she blushed further as she picked up her shirt, putting the hem in her mouth before putting her arms back out.

"Clever girl," Jaden praised. He hiked her up a bit higher and sucked one pert pink nipple into his mouth, his eyes never leaving hers. She moaned slightly and rocked her hips. He scraped his teeth over the bud and she cried out, throwing her head back against the wall with a thud.

"Lovely," he rasped. "Need to be inside you."

"Yes," she said around a gasp, dropping her shirt as she spoke.

"Stop me if it hurts you. I plan on having a lot more sex with you tonight and I don't want you in pain," Jaden said, shifting her in his arms as he fought to get his belt and jeans undone and down his thighs. His cock sprang out, throbbing in relief at its freedom. "Are you sure you're ready? I can play a bit more if you need me to." He flashed her a Cheshire grin like the cat that ate the canary.

Maddie chuckled. "I'm ready. Quit stalling."

Jaden shifted her thong to the side and thrust two fingers inside her, humming his appreciation as her juices coated his digits. She was right; she was dripping. She was so warm and tight. He couldn't wait to be inside her. He pulled out, making her whimper, and wiped his fingers over his cock, getting it slick for her. "Ready?" he asked her.

"Impale me," she begged.

Great choice of words.

Jaden angled her body so that the head of his cock caught on her opening.

Her legs were spread wide, her body pinned between his and the wall; with nowhere to go, she was at his mercy. And his mercy was slowly entering her tight little body, making her jaw go slack and eyes roll back in her head.

"Maddie, you feel so good around me," Jaden murmured when he could go no further. "Can I move, darling?"

"Move, yes! *Jaden!*" she cried on his first thrust. Her legs tightened around his hips, preventing him from pulling out too far, so he chose short, sharp thrusts that had her wailing in seconds.

"Not going to last long this first time. Come on, babe, come for me," Jaden gritted out between clenched teeth.

At his words, she came with a cry, her body arching in ecstasy. He followed her shortly after, her body milking him for every drop.

Panting, Maddie collapsed in his arms. Jaden carefully pulled out of her, making them both wince, and put her feet on the floor.

Jaden cupped her cheek, lifting her face until her blissed out eyes met his. He grinned at her. "Now that's a look I could get used to. To your room, but keep your skirt up. I want to watch your ass."

Maddie swallowed hard, her glittery blue eyes meeting his hazel ones.

He raised an eyebrow, waiting for her to move from his arms.

She rolled her eyes, turned on her heel, huffed out a breath, and then yanked her skirt up at the back before leading him up the stairs to her bedroom.

When they got into the room, he ordered her to stand in the middle and strip. "Feet apart, hands on the bed. Don't move," he said.

He found a washcloth in her linen closet and dumped her soap dish to hold the wet cloth. He returned to the bedroom to find her exactly how he'd left her.

"Good girl," he praised.

"I'm going to clean you up, and then I'm going to spank you as your punishment for rolling your eyes at me. After that, I'm going to fuck you into your mattress until you can't breathe. How does that sound?"

She shivered. "Delightful."

CHAPTER FIVE

JADEN STARED DOWN at Maddie's naked form on her bed. He'd cleaned her up, but when he'd left the room to rinse the cloth, he'd returned to her sound asleep. She was sprawled over the mattress, legs akimbo, her pussy still swollen.

Damn.

She'd actually fallen asleep after the last round of sex.

He huffed as his cock throbbed anew, wanting to rebury itself inside her gorgeous, silky heat once more.

Resolutely, he turned away from her, searching the floor for his discarded clothing. He might be a scoundrel, but he didn't fuck a sleeping woman without explicit consent.

Once dressed, he took one last look at her and then slipped down the stairs. The clock on the stove glowed two in the morning, and he stretched languidly. "Five-hour sex session, a new record," he whispered to himself. "Score."

Jaden slipped out the back door, since he didn't have the key to relock the front door, and sauntered down the street, humming to himself.

Augustine told me not to come back until I'd changed my attitude.

Mission accomplished.

He chuckled to himself and knew he had a grin plastered over his face from ear to ear.

Flashes of the evening passed through his thoughts; her ass, pink from the five, open-handed slaps he'd given each round globe. The expression on her face when he'd forced her to watch herself in the mirror as she rode him, legs spread wide over his thighs. She'd fit him like a glove, her body stretched to its limit. He didn't know how long he'd spent with his face buried between her strong thighs, or how many times she'd come on his tongue while he'd recovered his stamina, but he'd happily do it all again in a heartbeat.

All in all, it had been a fantastic evening of the best sex he'd ever had, and with a woman he really liked and connected with.

The house was dark, his brothers probably asleep, when he got home. He moved quietly up to his room, collapsing on his bed without even bothering to take off his shoes.

It felt like two seconds before Finley was shaking him awake.

"What did you do?" Finley hissed.

"Whaaaa?" Jaden mumbled. "Bed late. Sleeping in." He pulled the pillow over his head. "Go 'way."

"The cops are here for you," Finley said.

That woke Jaden up. "What? *Why?*"

"I asked you that."

"Nothing illegal, as far as I know." Jaden rolled out of bed, his thigh muscles protesting their use, and stripped out of his shirt. "I'll get to the bottom of this." He chose a fresh shirt and yanked it on, doing up the buttons as he thumped down the stairs.

"Mister Jaden McKellen?" one of the cops greeted him. "We need to ask you a few questions about your activities last night."

"Sure thing. What seems to be the problem, Officer?" Jaden sat on the couch opposite the two men in uniform. He noticed his brothers were hiding in the kitchen, pretending not to listen.

"After you left Valhalla's Throne, where did you go?"

"I came right back here to drop my gear and grab dinner," Jaden said, rubbing his chin thoughtfully. "My oldest brother and I got in a fight and I went back to the strip. I went to DeLux

Cafe and ended up stuck in that speed dating thing that Eve and Aphrodite run. Halfway through, a woman and I snuck out because she was hungry. We made it to ButterNut Bakery right before it closed. We ate in a park."

"What time was that?"

"Around eight."

"Hmm." The officer writing notes flipped back through his book. "I think we're going to have to bring you down to the station."

"Why? For skipping out on speed dating?" Jaden fought to keep his temper under control.

"Several witnesses heard you threaten to kill Pollux Begrond yesterday at Valhalla's Throne," the other officer said.

Jaden felt sick. "Pollux is dead?"

The officers stared at him grimly.

"What happened?"

"We can't divulge information about an active crime investigation," Note-taker said sharply. "Are you going to come with us willingly or are we going to have to arrest you?"

"I'll come with you willingly. I'm innocent." Jaden met his brothers' wide eyes, hoping they believed him.

The trip to the station was brief and silent. The officers, because it was their job. Jaden, because he didn't want to say anything that might implicate himself further.

He was brought to a room with a table and two chairs. He was told to sit and wait.

"Would it be possible to get a coffee?" Jaden asked. "I didn't get a chance for breakfast this morning."

"We'll see." They left him standing just inside the door.

Jaden looked around curiously. The table was simple, with a pair of metal loops to handcuff someone to it. The chairs were sturdy metal. Beyond that, there was a camera in the corner, which he gave a cheeky wave to, and a large mirror on one wall.

He took a good look at himself; he had obvious sex hair sticking up in all directions and the bruise on his eye was purpling nicely. He was tempted to encourage its healing, but worried that might make him look guilty.

More guilty?

I shouldn't have threatened Pollux.

I can't believe he's gone.

To force his mind off it, he decided to

go through his morning workout routine. He started off with sit-ups, the concrete floor hurting his spine until he thickened the skin over it with dragon scale.

He was proud that he managed to keep control over the minor transformation of his body. Augustine had been goading him to practice his shifting more often, but Jaden didn't like the memories it brought back. The ones of being hunted, driven from their home, desperate to find a way to hide until the world was more accepting of their kind. A witch had hidden them, put them in stasis, until a massive earthquake had shaken them awake. They'd lived in Purgatory ever since.

Augustine had ventured into the human world multiple times, even before he'd found his mate over half a year ago. He had told his brothers that the humans didn't notice him when he was in dragon form, that he could walk down the beach and nobody cared.

Jaden found that hard to believe.

How could anyone miss a giant purple dragon?

Each of the brothers had different colored scales; Augustine was purple, Finley was blue, and he was green. At any rate, he hadn't shifted fully in years. He barely remembered what it felt like to fly, to have the wind carry him, lift him...

He shook his head. No use dwelling on that now. His internal count for his sit-ups was nearing three hundred; when he reached that even number, he flipped onto his stomach and started doing push-ups.

Unfortunately, this position made him think about the gorgeous redhead he'd fucked so thoroughly the night before. He'd held himself over her in a position similar to this, but with a lot more hip thrusting.

All right, not only like this.

I also took her against the wall and on the edge of the bed, but I'm not getting visions of her while I stand or sit in a chair.

I hope.

That would be awkward; getting a hard-on while being questioned for murder.

At one hundred push-ups, the door to the room opened and Jaden saw a pair of shapely legs wearing heels enter the room. He got to his feet quickly, rubbing his dusty hands on the seat of his jeans before sticking one out to the woman. "Ma'am," he said respectfully.

She raised her eyebrow and shook his hand, her grip strong and sure. She handed him a bottle of water with her other hand. "Since you probably need it."

"Thanks." Jaden grinned and twisted the cap off, swallowing half of it in one gulp. "I usually do my workout in the morning. Didn't want to waste my time even more."

"You consider being here a waste of time?" the woman said, taking a seat at the table and gesturing at the chair across from her.

Jaden spun it around and sat with his forearms resting on the back of the chair. "I understand that you need to follow up on your leads. Murder is serious business," he said.

The woman's second eyebrow joined the first. "Murder *is* serious," she said blandly. "Have you murdered anyone?"

"Of course not!" Jaden fought to lower his voice. He took a deep breath. "I didn't like Pollux, that was no secret, but I kept it all in the ring, despite him wanting to fight me out of it. I didn't see him after our scheduled fight at six, but I have no idea how to prove that I *didn't* do something."

"I have eyewitness statements that say that Pollux was waiting for you after your match," the woman said calmly.

"My brother told me the same thing. Finley, I mean. He helped me sneak out the back door so that I wouldn't make things worse." Jaden shook his head. "I *am* sorry I made the threat, but it slipped out. He punched me in—" He stopped, remembering he was talking to a woman.

She grinned at him. "I saw footage of the fight. Caught you in the family jewels, didn't he?"

Jaden nodded sheepishly. "He lost a point for that cheap shot. You're not supposed to aim there."

"You didn't have that shiner last night," she said, indicating his left eye. "At least, not according to witnesses."

"I can tell you exactly when in the fight I got it," Jaden said. "I don't bruise easily, and when I do, it takes a while for them to show up."

"Did you know that DeLux Cafe is one of the public portals to the upper world?" she said, changing subjects.

"I did," Jaden said cautiously. "I

haven't been topside in years. No need to. Everything I want is here."

"Even women?"

"I have no problem getting a woman."

"Are you seeing anyone?"

"You're not my type," Jaden said with a lopsided smile and a wink.

The woman raised her eyebrow. "Not my question."

Jaden sighed inwardly. "I'm not in a serious relationship at this time."

"Is that why you went to the speed dating event?"

"Nope. I had no idea it was happening last night. I was in town to pick someone up for the evening, and a woman in a purple dress caught my eye as she entered the cafe. She turned out to be not my type, but I stuck around for a while anyway, to see if anyone else might be.”

"Any luck?"

"I don't kiss and tell."

The woman looked unimpressed. "Might I remind you of where you are currently sitting?"

Jaden scowled. "I'd rather get myself out of this mess without dragging anyone else into it, thank you very much."

"Do you know where Pollux lives?" she asked, changing subjects again.

"Not a clue. We weren't exactly buddy-buddy, you know. I avoided him as much as possible. He was a bully, not to speak ill of the dead." Jaden shifted in his seat. The chairs were as uncomfortable as they looked.

The woman sat in silence for a moment. "I need a coffee. Want anything?”

“A coffee would be great, please.”

She went to the door and knocked on it, leaving him alone again. He sighed and flipped the chair around, putting his head down on the table. It was going to be a long day, he could tell.

The woman came back with a tray. On it were two coffees and little cream and sugar packets. “Make it however you like it.”

“Thanks,” Jaden said, pulling one cup toward him and dumping four cream and six sugars into it. He stirred it with one of the little sticks and sipped. “That’s good. Tastes like ButterNut Bakery coffee.”

“That’s because it is.” The woman regarded him over the rim of her cup. “I’m on loan from up above, because this crime took place in L.A., not Purgatory. Since I live here, I was the obvious choice to be the liaison."

"Okay." Jaden frowned, confused. "Why are you telling me this?"

"Well, for one, you don't seem to recognize me, even though we've met before."

Jaden examined her face, trying to think of where he might have seen her before. Finally the pieces clicked into place. "My lady," he said, giving her a seated bow. "Sorry, I didn't recognize you."

"It was a refreshing change," Chloe said dryly. She leaned forward, putting her cup down and resting her elbows on the table. "Why do you think Pollux was murdered?"

"My guess is he pissed off the wrong

people," Jaden said. "He was pretty great at doing that."

Chloe shook her head. "You misunderstand. Why do you think he was *murdered*?"

Jaden frowned. "He doesn't seem like the kind of guy that would commit suicide, especially after he won a match."

Rubbing her temples, Chloe chuckled softly. "Mister McKellen. Jaden. Pollux isn't dead. Why do you think he is?"

"He's not?" Jaden gaped at her. "But the officers that came to my house said..." He paused, thinking back over their conversation. "They let me think he was dead. I jumped to that conclusion because that's what my threat had been." He huffed impatiently. "Okay, great, I can go on thinking he's a miserable bastard. Why the fuck was I brought here if he's not dead?"

"Because his home was turned upside down and he was beaten within an inch of his life," Chloe said softly. "And after losing to him, quite badly, I might add, you are our prime suspect."

"Well, shit." Jaden rubbed his chin. "I don't know where he lives, but I can't prove I don't know something. He's certainly on my shit list, but I do *not* go looking for fights outside the ring. There are rules at Odin's for a reason. But you are right, I would have been capable of serving him up the beating of his life. The fact remains that I did *not*," Jaden paused meaningfully, "and would *never* do that, even to Pollux."

"I want to believe you," Chloe said. "But as you so succinctly point out, you are our prime suspect. Therefore…" She crossed her arms. "You need to provide us with your alibi."

Jaden rolled his head on his neck, cursing Augustine for kicking him out of the house last night in ancient Greek in his head. "Do you have a timeframe?"

"Between seven and eleven."

He groaned. "It's not enough to say that I have an alibi?"

"That's not how this works," Chloe said, unimpressed with his reluctance to come forward.

"All right, all right. At seven, I was at DeLux Cafe for speed dating. Aphrodite and Eve can prove I was there. At seven-thirty, I met this woman who said she was hungry and wanted to leave. She wanted to sneak out like James Bond, so I provided her cover by tripping one of the other guys and generally being a nuisance. We went out by the kitchen. I'm not sure if any of the chefs paid attention to us, but we were seen by several of them."

Chloe made a note on a piece of paper he hadn't seen her pull out. "Go on."

"We went to ButterNut Bakery. Demi was working. We didn't stay because it was almost closing, and went to the park."

"Which park?"

"I don't know, the one with the slides and the swings. We sat on a bench and ate. Flirting became a bit more intense and she asked me back to her place. I won't go into details about what we did there—"

"You don't have to," Chloe reassured him.

"But I left at two. I remember the time because I was impressed. At that point I don't believe anyone saw me, but I went straight home and fell into bed. My brothers were not awake," Jaden concluded.

"So this woman, who you still have not named, is the only person who can guarantee your whereabouts during the timeframe I gave you." She gave him a sympathetic look. "I'm going to need her name."

"I only know her first name."

"That gives me something to go on," Chloe said encouragingly.

Jaden blew out a long breath. "Maddie."

"Describe her," Chloe said.

"Curly red hair, blue eyes, curves to die for—" Jaden snapped his mouth shut. "She works with kids at a daycare. Is that enough?"

"That's sufficient," Chloe said. "You'll remain here in the meantime. I'll see that someone brings you food. If you need to use the toilet, knock on the door and you will be escorted. *Don't* abuse the privilege."

Jaden raised his hands. "I'm doing my best to cooperate."

Chloe raised an eyebrow silently and left the room.

The time passed, whether slowly or quickly Jaden wasn't sure, as there was no clock in the room and he didn't have his phone with him. Someone did bring him a sandwich, from ButterNut Bakery at that. It was his favorite, too, ham and swiss on rye.

"Thank you, Hera," Jaden mumbled

to himself around his first bite. Hera was his brother Augustine's mate, and she worked with her sister, Demi, at the bakery.

Getting this sandwich was like a message saying, "We believe in you!"

One he desperately needed right now.

He hoped Chloe could find Maddie. He hoped Maddie wasn't too pissed at him for leaving in the middle of the night. Jaden winced.

This is going to be so fucking awkward.

It was plenty of time for him to stew over the impending meeting with his one night stand when he didn't want to see her again.

His thoughts fought back over that.

After a night of sex that epic I don't want to see her again?

What am I thinking?

He scoffed to himself.

I don't do relationships, remember?

I can find another woman to have amazing sex with.

He didn't like how unsure he sounded, even to himself.

Women make everything about emotions and shit gets messy.

I don't want to deal with that.

Maybe I want to deal with it, if it's Maddie.

I didn't exactly give her a head's up about how the night was going to go.

"Shut up," he groaned, burying his face in his hands.

He looked up when the door opened. It remained open and Chloe stood to one side, expressionless. "Your alibi checks out, Mister McKellen. Thank you for cooperating today."

"I hope you catch whoever did it," Jaden said, getting to his feet.

"If you have any idea who it might be, please give me a call." Chloe handed him a card. "Otherwise, I hope we don't cross paths again."

"Professionally," Jaden added with a wink.

Chloe shot him a glare. "In any capacity."

"Understood." Jaden nodded sharply, wondering what he'd done to piss her off.

That question was answered when Chloe escorted him out, greeting a beautiful redhead standing at a desk with a hug.

Ah, shit.

His heart lurched at the sight of Maddie's gorgeous red hair and delicious curves. He supposed he should be grateful that she hadn't decided to make him sweat a little longer.

He tucked the card into his pocket and tried to be inconspicuous as he walked out.

It was not to be.

Maddie said goodbye and reached the exit at the same time as he did.

Jaden opened the door with a little bow. "After you," he murmured.

She raised an eyebrow and walked past him without a word.

He considered letting her go, but she *had* come down to clear his name. Biting back a groan of frustration, he jogged after her. "Maddie—"

She whirled to face him. "What is so important to say that you couldn't have stayed to tell me this morning?"

"Thank you," he said. He clarified further, "For coming here. I didn't want to drag you into this mess—"

"You're welcome." Maddie turned smartly on her heel.

Jaden watched her walk away, annoyed, both with himself for leaving her bed and her for being so...

So emotional.

"Bah," he said, and started jogging home.

Finley was still home, Augustine having gone to work. "How was it?"

Glaring at him as he opened the fridge, Jaden didn't bother responding.

"Okay, let me rephrase. Are we harboring a criminal?" Finley teased.

"Fin, I'm not in the mood. All I've had to eat since yesterday's dinner was a pretzel and a sandwich," Jaden growled.

"Leftovers from dinner are in the oven," Finley said.

"You're a lifesaver," Jaden said with relief, pulling out the warm plate of chicken pasta.

"I thought you might want something hot after a day of being raked over the coals," Finley teased.

"Still not in the mood. Talk after I've eaten."

"Can I see your prison tattoo?"

"Shut the fuck up."

CHAPTER SIX

ONE WEEKEND PASSED, and then another. Maddie was *still* angry. At Jaden, at herself, at all the circumstances that led to... well, everything.

She'd been avoiding Chloe, which wasn't as difficult as she'd thought it would be. Lucifer had been picking up Atlanta, which made Maddie feel even worse.

What Chloe must think of me!

I'm so embarrassed!

But today was a new day, and she firmly removed Jaden from her mind as she walked to work. She got there before Hestia, and did the security check around the backyard before unlocking the main door. Hestia arrived not much later, and they prepared for the day, talking quietly about the kids and what they hoped to do that day.

"Maddie!" exclaimed Alexander when he burst into the daycare.

"Alexander!" she replied back in the same tone. "What's up, buddy?"

"Me practicing mine handstands!"

"Have you? Do you want to show me your handstands?" Maddie bit back a giggle, the child's enthusiasm and antics making the negative thoughts plaguing her drift away.

Alexander carefully checked around himself before bending over and putting his hands on the floor, feet still firmly planted on the ground. Then he popped up again, all smiles. "Did you see mine handstand?" he shouted excitedly.

"I sure did!" Maddie avoided eye contact with his mother, who had followed him in, sure she would break out into laughter if she saw her amusement. "You got your hands right down on the ground!"

"Yes!"

Damien entered next, a little more sedately, and the boys hugged before heading off in different directions for their favorite toys.

"Don't take out too much, boys," Maddie told them. "It's going to rain this afternoon, so we're going to play outside this morning instead."

"Okay, Maddie," Damien said, putting back all but the Stegosaurus.

"Thank you." Maddie turned to the other adult. "Everything good?"

"Actually..." Alexander's mother winced. "I was hoping you might have a suggestion."

"About?" Maddie prodded.

"He's not telling us what he needs at home. He gets upset and throws a tantrum if I don't understand his gestures."

Maddie nodded thoughtfully. "He's got enough words to be able to tell you anything he needs. I think I might have a book about communicating that might help him. I'll read it this afternoon."

"Oh, thank you!" Alexander's mother

gushed as she left. "I really appreciate it."

"No problem!" Maddie greeted Shana's mother, who had just arrived, taking the child from her with a smile. "Have a good day."

A woman dropped Lyta's backpack just inside the door. "I'll try," she said with a weary sigh.

"Start with your mindset," Maddie advised. "You'll get through this day one minute at a time."

"One second at a time," Lyta's mother grumbled. "It was a hard night."

"Did you give Mummy a hard time, Baby?" Maddie cooed to the little girl. "We'll see what we can do for your teeth today, shall we?"

Lyta scrunched up her face, two big fat tears trickling down her cheeks.

"Sweetheart," Maddie said, her heart melting. She hugged the baby to her chest. "Maybe you should take an hour nap and then head to work," she suggested to the woman. "You'll be more prepared to tackle the day.

"That sounds amazing." Lyta's mother brightened. "I'll call in while I head home. You're a genius."

"I know." Maddie grinned and closed the door behind her. "Let's get you a frozen teether, hmm?"

More silent tears fell.

"What do you say about a nice foot massage from Hestia? She's been studying pressure points and might be able to get rid of some of that pain." Maddie carried the baby to the kitchen, dug her teether out of the freezer, and handed both over to Hestia just in time to welcome the last parent.

It wasn't Lucifer.

Maddie greeted Atlanta without looking at Chloe, afraid of what she'd see in the detective's gaze.

"It has been far too long," Chloe said. "This case has got me running around like a chicken without a head, if you can believe it."

"I'm sorry to hear that," Maddie replied, taking the baby from her.

"Every lead we have dries up like Ilia." Chloe sighed, obviously frustrated. "Must be a professional hit, but why would it be on one of the fighters at Odin's?" She shook her head. "Sorry to bother you with all this. Forget I said anything. How are you?"

Maddie stared for a second. "Miserable," she said at last, and then wished she could take the word back.

Chloe frowned, upset. "I have to get to work, but when I pick Atlanta up, we can chat about that. I've missed you." She gave Maddie a tight hug and kissed her daughter's head, running her hand through the baby's thin hair. "Have a good day."

"You too," Maddie replied. She was a little confused; Chloe seemed genuinely concerned about her.

It's been a while since I had a friend, I guess.

"Why don't we all head outside and learn how to do a somersault?" she said to the delighted children. She was grateful that she'd decided to wear leggings this morning.

The morning was full of hilarity, grass stains, and triumphs. Damien already knew how to do a somersault, so Maddie started teaching him cartwheels. Alexander could manage a somersault by the end of their time outside, and proudly did a set of three in a row across the lawn just to prove he could. Lyta enjoyed watching, but wasn't interested in leaving Hestia's lap, or the shade that they were sitting underneath.

Atlanta, the instant she was placed on the ground, half-transformed into her usual wolf-demon form. She rocked back and forth on her hind paws and hands, screeching whenever one of the boys ran by her.

"Put your head down," Damien suggested to her at one point. "Then you'll tumble forward and you'll do the somersault!"

"Unfortunately, she's too little to

understand," Maddie said comfortingly when Damien started getting frustrated that she wasn't doing what he said.

"Like this!" Alexander said, demonstrating again in front of the baby.

Atlanta shrieked and moved forward a step.

"You did it! You crawled!" Maddie said excitedly. She crouched in front of the baby. "Come here, sweetie."

Atlanta grinned a gummy smile and moved robotically forward again until she fell on her nose and the rest of her transformed in a blink into a wolf. She howled, picked herself up, and trotted the rest of the way to Maddie for comfort.

Maddie's jaw dropped as she sat down. "You just transformed! You did it! And then you walked!" She cradled the baby in her arms, rubbing her hands through the soft fur on the baby's belly. In a second, she was holding the human form of Atlanta again. "I'm so proud of you!" Maddie said happily. "You did it all by yourself!"

The baby burbled cheerfully, so obviously proud of herself that the adults chuckled.

"I think it's time for snacks and quiet time," Maddie said, repeating the phrase that started their calm down routine.

Forty minutes later, all four kids were asleep in various locations. Lyta had cried until Maddie wrapped her to her chest and walked around the yard, the constant motion finally soothing the baby to sleep.

"Poor thing," Maddie had murmured to Hestia when she'd entered the building. She sat in the rocking chair with Lyta still on her, keeping up with the constant motion, and pulled out her phone to text Chloe.

Atlanta fully shifted into a wolf this morning.

She didn't have to wait long for a response.

You're kidding! That's amazing!

Maddie smiled. *She fell flat on her face and then poof! Wolf puppy.*

Aww, I can't wait to see her!

The rest of the day was uneventful, in the way one would hope a full day with kids cooped up inside can be. Maddie read the book about communication being a two-way street she'd promised to the boys. Only time would tell whether Alexander had understood its message.

Chloe was the last parent to collect

their child. Maddie was concerned at the lateness, thinking that perhaps Lucifer would come instead, that Chloe had forgotten her promise.

"You're coming for dinner," Chloe said, entering the building with a gust of wind full of rain.

"Am I?" Maddie teased.

"You are. We need more time than I can give before a meal. This one is always hungry," Chloe said, making faces at Atlanta. "I hear you became a full wolf, my daughter! I'm very proud of you!"

"Only once, I'm afraid," Maddie said apologetically. "She didn't do the full shift again this afternoon."

Chloe brushed her concerns aside. "She will. It just takes practice. Can you come now, or do you need to close up here?"

"I've got this," Hestia said. "Go ahead."

Maddie shrugged. "I'm all yours."

"Great." Chloe strapped Atlanta to her back with quick efficiency and picked up her discarded umbrella. "Once more into the breach!" she said, opening the door.

The rain hadn't tapered off at all, making Maddie wonder if it was a supernaturally caused storm like those they had a while back when Hera was down in the dumps over her mate. They walked side by side under their umbrellas until they reached Lucifer's home. Maddie was mildly intimidated by its size, but obediently followed Chloe into the foyer, dripping water onto the polished floors.

Lucifer entered from a hallway not

long after they had put away their umbrellas, greeting his wife with a kiss and took the baby from her back. "It is time for your dinner, Miss," he told the baby, tickling her belly with his face. He wrinkled his nose. "And a change." He vanished as quickly as he'd appeared.

"Shall we adjourn to the parlor?" Chloe asked, a twinkle in her eye.

"You have a parlor?" Maddie countered. "I'm not even sure what a parlor *is*."

"A living room," Chloe said with a chuckle. She arched her back, stretching her arms over her head. "Ugh, it's good to be home."

The parlor was a comfortable room with a soft looking sofa and lots of books.

"I think I'd be tempted to call this a

library," Maddie said, looking around.

"Oh no, the library has way more books," Chloe said. "These are just the ones that Lucifer deems 'fancy' and puts out to impress callers."

Maddie giggled. "I'm certainly getting a different impression of Lucifer from you than I did from my introduction to him several years ago."

Chloe smiled. "I've been told I'm a good influence." She sat on the sofa and patted the seat beside her. "Spill. Why are you miserable?"

"No beating around the bush, huh?" Maddie said.

"I do that enough at work," Chloe replied, rubbing her temples. "I'm much more blunt at home because of it."

"Okay." Maddie sucked in a deep breath. "It's about the speed dating thing.”

Chloe nodded, giving nothing away with her expression.

“I regret going,” Maddie blurted out.

“Why?”

“Because if I hadn’t gone, I wouldn’t have met *him*.”

Chloe nodded thoughtfully for a moment after that. “You think you’d be happier if you hadn’t met him?”

“Well, yeah.” Maddie huffed, crossing her arms and leaning back on the cushions. “Or maybe what I regret is leaving with him.”

“How many speed dates had you been on before you met him?” Chloe asked.

“Five or six.”

“What did you think of them?”

“Stuffy bores,” Maddie said bluntly.

Chloe chuckled. “And the

aforementioned 'him?' What did you think of him?"

Maddie blushed. "Exciting. New. Hot."

"If you didn't know what would happen after, would you still leave with him if you could go back in time?"

"Ugh, that's hard." Maddie closed her eyes, resting her head on the back of the couch. "Yes. Yes, I probably would."

"Why?"

"What do you mean, why?" Maddie asked. She turned her face away, her cheeks burning. "I'm sure you heard all about how the evening went from *him*. I could see it in his eyes the moment we met. I wouldn't turn that away. Couldn't."

"Maddie, what exactly— No, scratch that." Chloe hummed to herself for a moment, and then took Maddie's hands in hers. "Look at me. Jaden—stop it and listen to me very carefully—Jaden didn't even mention you until he absolutely *had to*. He only told your name to me, not to the officers who picked him up. The only details he gave were that he left at two, when he went home."

Maddie shook her head, tears pricking her eyes. "But *why* did he leave?"

"He didn't tell me that," Chloe said. "But I'm serious, Maddie. He tried to keep you out of it. We needed to know his whereabouts between seven and eleven, and he was with you for the bulk of that. Otherwise, I'm sure he wouldn't have even mentioned you."

Now Maddie was annoyed with herself. "Why am I even more bothered by that? Was I so unmentionable?" she asked, blowing her bangs out of her eyes.

Chloe smiled sympathetically. "When I asked him to describe you, he was very complimentary."

Maddie couldn't think of a response to that. She tightened her lips and closed her eyes again.

"I really think you need to go talk to him," Chloe said gently.

"Even if I wanted to, I don't know anything about him," Maddie said.

"Lucky for you, I do." Chloe grinned. "The rain should have cleared by the time we finish eating. After dinner, here's what you're going to do. You're going to go home, put on something cute, and then you're going to go to Valhalla's Throne. Either he or his brothers will be on the schedule tonight. If it's Augustine or Finley, you can ask them for their address. If it's Jaden, you can have your chat. Ask him why he left in the middle of the night and then didn't mention you during a police investigation."

"Do you really think that'll work?" Maddie managed to stop herself from whining just in time. "What if he's the kind of guy who's one-and-done?"

"Then you deserve to hear that to your face, don't you think?" Chloe replied. She twisted her mouth up in consideration. "Actually, don't put on something cute. Put on something drop dead gorgeous. He's already seen you in 'cute.'"

Maddie laughed in spite of herself. "I don't have anything like that."

"Okay, I'm going to make a call." Chloe winked at her as she held her cell up to her ear. "It helps to have a Goddess on speed dial. Hera? It's Chloe. Are you with Augustine tonight? Do you mind taking a few minutes to help out a friend? She needs to re-seduce Jaden. He's at Odin's at eight? That's perfect. Yeah, come by my place in about an hour? You're the best. Love you, too. Mwah." Chloe beamed at Maddie. "Your personal stylist will arrive after dinner. And she knows Jaden, so she knows what'll make him fall at your feet."

"How will that help us talk?"

"That's *your* job. First, you've got to make Jaden wake up and notice you. We got you, girl."

Maddie swallowed nervously. "Thanks. I think."

CHAPTER SEVEN

HERA ARRIVED IMMEDIATELY following dinner, just as she promised, and she'd brought Arachne with her. Maddie loved the clothes she'd seen created by the woman who owned Metamorphosis but she'd never owned any of the spider shifter's unique creations herself so this, having the talented woman here to help make her look delectable enough to seduce Jaden, was a definite treat. Chloe whisked all three women up to a spare bedroom.

"Do you want to keep the clothes you're currently wearing?" Arachne asked, eyeing Maddie appreciatively.

"These are my favorite leggings," Maddie said tentatively.

"Strip off everything you want to keep as-is," Arachne ordered. "I do need to work some with material that already exists, though."

"Um. Okay." Maddie sat on the edge of the bed and pulled off her leggings before standing awkwardly in front of the women again. "Where do you want me?"

"You're good where you are." Arachne circled her slowly. "Do you prefer loose or tight clothing?"

"Loose, please."

"All right then." Arachne flexed her fingers and grinned.

"Your fairy godmothers are ready to work their magic." Hera quipped with a smile crossing her face.

"Do you say 'bibbidi bobbidi' or something?" Maddie said with a chuckle to hide her nerves.

Arachne touched her shoulder, waving her hands over Maddie's chest faster than she could even keep track of, and changed her simple blue t-shirt into a sheer peasant blouse with a wide neck.

"Hmm," the woman said thoughtfully, and then put a cool finger against Maddie's bra strap. The material flickered through the blue blouse and reappeared, forming a flexible underbust corset.

Maddie's cheeks flared as red as her

hair. "But..." She gestured at her fully visible breasts.

"Odin's is dimly lit. Nobody'll notice," Hera reassured her. She winked. "At least until you get in front of Jaden."

"The point is to *talk* to him," Maddie protested. "How can I talk to him if he's not paying attention to my words?"

Hera raised her eyebrow. "I thought you were re-seducing him and then pulling away to talk to him?"

Maddie bit her lip. "I'm not sure I'll be able to stop."

Three women smirked at her. "That good, huh?"

"You have *no idea*," Maddie groaned, covering her face with her hands.

"I have a pretty good idea," Hera said. "His brother *is* my mate." She examined Maddie again. "But if you're not comfortable…”

“Maybe if it was a little less sheer?” Maddie suggested.

“Very well.” Another brush of Arachne's fingertips over her shoulders and the shirt thickened slightly.

Maddie examined herself in the mirror over the dresser. She couldn't see her nipples unless the light hit the material at just the right angle. “Thank you. Much better,” she said, relieved.

“Now for your lower half.” Arachne tapped her lips. “A jean skirt, perhaps? Something form-fitting to contrast with the flowiness of the top.”

“That sounds good,” Maddie agreed.

“Perfect.” Hera grinned mischievously and Maddie didn't understand why until she felt the shift of her clothing.

“But—” she started to say.

"You wanted to keep your leggings," Hera reminded her, a twinkle in her eye.

Maddie swallowed hard, meeting Chloe's gaze.

Chloe chuckled. "It'll be easier for makeup sex after your chat," she said, shrugging.

"I suppose," Maddie said dubiously. She rolled up her leggings and tucked them into her purse.

After saying their goodbyes to Chloe and Arachne at the door—Lucifer had disappeared and Atlanta was asleep so Arachne and Chloe were taking the rare opportunity to catch up on a little girl time—Maddie and Hera walked down the street toward Valhalla's Throne.

"Do you know what you're going to say?" Hera asked after they'd walked in silence for a few minutes.

"Something like, 'Why did you leave?' I guess," Maddie replied.

"Oh honey, no." Hera shook her head. "You need to be assertive."

Maddie bit her lip as she thought. "I can do that. I hope."

"I have no doubts," Hera said, giving her a hug. "This is me. *You* have fun tonight." She winked.

Blushing, Maddie wished her well and turned down the street where she would find the underground fight club. She'd never been there before, and swallowed her nerves as the businesses on either side of the street became dingier the closer she got to the club, their neon lights illuminating the street in a mix of reds, blues, and yellows that did it no favors.

She spotted the metal door at the

bottom of a set of stairs and slowly descended them. She was just about to knock the rhythm that Chloe had taught her when a group of large men crowded behind her.

The man at the front knocked on the door beside her raised fist, getting uncomfortably into her space. He sniffed her hair. "Ain't you a pretty thing," he drawled in her ear. "I've got the perfect seat for that little ass of yours." He ran his hand over the body part in question, making the other men behind her whoop and cheer.

Before Maddie could say a word, the sliding grate at eye level opened. It closed just as quickly, before she could even say the password she'd been given, and the door opened, the creak as loud as her heartbeat pounding in her ears.

She was swept into the hallway beyond the door by the men, not even getting a chance to see the bouncer.

How am I going to get away from these guys?.

"I'm looking forward to feeling what you've got underneath that sexy skirt of yours," the man immediately behind her said, his hand getting lower on her leg.

"I need to freshen up," Maddie said suddenly, spying the sign for the bathrooms off the main corridor.

"Don't be too long, little Ruby," the man said. "Else I'll have to come looking for you."

A security guard passed by them, nodding at the men and completely ignoring her.

A sinking feeling hit her belly. She'd have no help there.

"I'll be just fine," she whispered to herself. Maddie walked quickly down the new hallway, relieved that she heard no footsteps following her. This new hallway continued past the bathrooms, and several closed doors. She followed the passage to a set of stairs that went down. She took them, eager to explore and discover where she'd end up.

The cheering and sounds of bodies hitting each other started to get louder, and she wondered whether she was going to come out inside the fighting ring when she came to the end of journey. The stairs ended in another hallway, this one wider and shorter than the last with several more closed doors sparsely interspersed down its path. There were men and women in fighting gear stretching on the floor or against the walls between the doors. Through an open space at the end, she could see the fight going on in the ring. She backed up into the hallway, not wanting to be seen. In doing so, she noticed a door on her right. She opened it a crack, peering through, and saw that it led to the lowest ring of bleachers. Sticking to the shadows, she slipped through the door and found a seat, wishing she could cover her hair.

The auditorium was rounded, with seats rising like the ancient amphitheaters of Greece, so that everyone could see what happened in the central fighting ring. This close to the action, Maddie was worried that the men who had come in with her might catch a glimpse of her while looking at the ring. Unfortunately, she hadn't seen them, only heard the one man's voice and felt his hand on her, so she couldn't watch out for them. As it was, a spectator looking at the audience instead of the fight would be remarkable, so she had to maintain appearances.

Maddie finally focused on the fighters, her heart still thundering unpleasantly hard from her uncomfortable experience.

And then it beat quicker for an entirely different reason, for Jaden was one of the fighters.

He seemed to be winning, from her inexperienced opinion. At least, the other guy looked pretty bruised and didn't seem like he'd last much longer. Jaden ducked under a wild punch, following up with a grapple that brought the other guy to his knees.

After a bit of a struggle, the other guy tapped the sand with an open palm and a third man entered the ring with a microphone. "Jaden 'J-Star' McKellen is the winner!" he declared to raucous applause.

Jaden helped the other man to his feet before shaking his hand and they headed out of the ring.

Maddie quickly climbed to her feet, relieved that she didn't have to stay there any longer, and exited by the same door she'd entered. Jaden was helping his opponent limp across the ready room, both men waving away assistance from the other fighters.

A fresh round of applause filtered through the space, indicating a new fighter was being introduced.

Watching for her chance to follow

Jaden, she waited until they'd gone down another hallway to the right and the other fighters weren't paying attention to anything but the new fight before she slipped from her hallway into the new one.

She hurried down it, hoping they hadn't gone far, when she saw Jaden ahead of her, leaning against the open door of a room.

"See the doc, rest up. You need to work on your footwork, man," Jaden said.

The response was muffled to Maddie's ears, but Jaden chuckled.

"When you can beat me consistently, then you'll know you're good enough." Jaden backed out of the doorway, closing the solid wooden door behind him, and started walking down the hallway at a pace that had Maddie jogging to keep up. Finally, he reached another door and opened it.

Maddie ran the last few steps and followed him into the room. "You have a lot of explaining to do, Mister McKellen," she said sternly, startling him into a yelp and a quick turn on his heel to face her.

The guilty look on his face made her even angrier. She kept walking, backing him up against the wall beside the shower. When he had nowhere else to go, she stopped and poked him in the chest with one finger. "What do you have to say for yourself?"

Jaden's mouth opened and closed.

She raised an eyebrow and crossed her arms under her breasts.

His gaze dropped from her face to her chest and he groaned. "Gods, Maddie.

You look amazing."

Her heart rate picked up and she blushed. "No, that's not—" She cut herself off when he lifted a large hand, so warm she could feel over her skin it even without contact. He held it between them, hovering, not touching. Her breaths were coming faster now, her chest heaving with each intake, getting closer to him.

"Maddie," he murmured. "What do you want?"

Questions ran through her mind in a split second.

Why did you leave?

Why didn't you brag about our night together?

Why did you treat me the way you did at the station?

Only to be crowded out by one

thought:

He's still waiting for consent to touch me.

That decided it.

"You," she whispered.

Jaden groaned, his hand shaking. "Say it."

It took her a moment. "Please, touch me, Jaden."

He immediately closed the distance between his hand and her breast, palming the small mound. "Fuck, Maddie," he rasped. "Your body is so beautiful."

Her only response was a whimper as he teased at her already hard nipples.

When did that happen?

Then he bent and suckled her breast through the thin material and she didn't care about timing any more. All she cared about was getting this man inside her as fast as possible.

He pulled back, running his thumb over the wet splotch he'd made on her shirt. "Maddie, what you do to me, baby."

"Lock the door. I need you," Maddie barked in reply.

Jaden's eyebrows rose along with the corner of his mouth. "I haven't been able to get you out of my mind. Are you sure this isn't just another fantasy?"

"Do you want me to slap you?" Maddie asked.

"Isn't it usually a pinch?"

"Not when the guy in question left in the middle of the night."

"Fair enough. No slaps needed." Jaden backed her up until they reached the door. He closed it and flicked the deadbolt over. "No one will bother us now. Are you sure you don't want me to shower first?"

"I'll shower with you after and we can go again."

Jaden smirked. "Impatient."

"Very. And you still haven't kissed me."

"Can't have that." Jaden picked her up by her thighs and put her down on the table, kicking the chair out of the way. He stepped between her spread legs and devoured her mouth, one big hand securing the back of her head as he mapped out her lips, teeth, and tongue with his.

Her head was spinning with desire. She could barely think.

Why did I come here again?

That thought was swept away as

easily as her breasts were bared to his free hand, the gauzy material pulled down and tucked under them.

"So sexy," Jaden muttered. "I could see your hard little nipples through your shirt the instant you walked through my door. You're never allowed to wear a bra again. I want easy access to these every minute of the day." He bent and scraped his teeth over one bud and then the other, squeezing her breasts together one moment and then twisting her nipples the next while he plundered her mouth again.

"Jaden!" Maddie gasped when he released her. Her thighs were shaking, she was so turned on.

"I've got you, babe," Jaden growled, his hands leaving her body to remove his fighting shorts, black with green scales down the sides, and unstrap his cup. His hard cock sprang free, slapping his belly. "Lift your ass," he said, working her skirt up her thighs while showering her neck with open-mouthed kisses. "Need to be right up against you. Feel your heat through your panties."

"Yesssss," Maddie moaned, throwing her head back, exposing her throat to his explorations. A second later, her bare ass was on the table and she suddenly remembered a crucial missing garment. But there was no time to tell—warn?—Jaden before his cock was against her wet folds and they both sucked in an involuntary breath.

"Darlin'," Jaden murmured, his lips curving into a smirk on her skin. "Did you come see me at work wearing nothing underneath that tight-fitting skirt of yours?" He ground against her, making her gasp.

"Arachne..." Maddie swallowed hard, closing her eyes to try to concentrate. "Arachne said that— Jaden, oh my *god* don't stop doing that—" She held his head to her pulse point with one hand, her hips rocking unconsciously.

"What did Arachne say?" Jaden asked after it was clear that Maddie wasn't going to continue her thought.

"She said that she can only transform something that already exists, and I wanted to keep my leggings. They're my favorites." Maddie pouted when Jaden stopped kissing her neck to stare at her.

"That's not true. I've seen her create things mid-air," he said.

Maddie's jaw dropped. "You're kidding."

"I'll have to think of a way to thank her," Jaden said with a grin. "Best gift ever. Come here, bend over and face the mirror. Yes, hands on the table, that's it. Fuck—" He ran his hands over her exposed flesh, starting with her ass before covering her body with his and cupping her swaying breasts in his hands. His cock nudged at her slick folds, the head slipping easily through them and catching on her opening. "Babe, can I—"

"I need you inside me!" Maddie almost wailed, meeting his gaze with hers in the mirror.

He grinned, the amusement written all over his face making her embarrassed and angry, but then he shifted his hips slightly, his hands coming to rest on the table on either side of hers.

Her eyes closed at the pleasure of being split open by his cock, but then he stopped moving. "More, please!" she begged.

"I want you to watch yourself," Jaden ordered. "You're so beautiful when you're aroused." When she opened her eyes, he continued both entering her and his words, "Look how flushed you are. Your chest is red, your nipples tight. You're so wet, your thighs are dripping with it. Everything about you is screaming your arousal, and baby, I'm going to make sure you come so hard you'll feel it in every nerve of your body."

Her back arched, she went up on her tiptoes, trying to get closer to him, to get him to fill her faster, to get him balls-deep within her.

"You don't get to move," he half-growled, nipping at her shoulder. His hands left the table and hauled her up by her hips, her feet leaving the floor, all her weight on her hands. "You want to feel me deep inside you?" He finished his thrust, snapping his hips into her so hard that his balls swung forward and hit her clit.

Maddie shouted her pleasure, egging him on. He adjusted his hold on her and started up a fast rhythm that had her shaking with her first orgasm of the night in seconds.

"Oh yeah, baby, come apart for me and I'll put you back together again," Jaden grunted. He put her down and flipped her over, putting the edge of her ass on the table and sliding home again before she'd finished coming down from her high. "I can feel every inch of you screaming out for me," he said, pounding into her wanton channel.

Maddie clung to his solid arms, her fingernails digging in to his biceps as he took her on the wildest ride of her life. All too soon, she felt the next wave of pleasure cresting, her body taut like a bowstring before release.

"Come for me, Maddie," he whispered in her ear, and that was all it took.

Ripples of pleasure coursing through her, she crested and then fell apart with a scream, her core clutching around his length. She sucked gulps of air, sweat cooling on her skin.

Jaden was still hard within her, pulsing his hips in incremental movements that told her he was close but wanted to draw out her pleasure.

Maddie sat up, making them both

groan as he shifted within her. Her lips traced the shell of his ear and then she murmured, "Come inside me. Mark me as yours," and bit down where his shoulder met neck.

Jaden let himself go with a roar that made her ears ring, his hips pumping inside her.

He braced his arms on either side of her hips, muscles twitching as he panted for breath. "Fuck, Maddie," he rasped. "Feels like you sucked me dry."

"Shower?" she suggested.

Jaden nodded. He pulled out and Maddie whimpered at the loss, making him grin. His cock twitched and she smiled.

"Not so dry, are you?"

"I should've known better than to assume," Jaden admitted. He backed away from her, moving over to the shower. "Mildly warm, warm, or intensely cold?"

Maddie chuckled, stripping out of her clothes as fast as possible. "Are those the only options?"

"Unfortunately."

"Let's go for warm."

"I always try for that. Doesn't always work out," Jaden muttered, and the hiss of the pipes filled the little room.

She traced her fingers over Jaden's broad shoulders, smoothing the soft skin and counting the pale freckles that only showed up when he exerted himself. The light brown showed up on the reddened skin, but blended into his natural skin tone.

Maddie pressed kisses to his chest as high as she could reach. She flicked her tongue over his nipple and his breath caught in his throat. "You could be a model," she purred. "Just stand in the corner of my room all day and look pretty."

Jaden chuckled. "Not likely."

"A model for an upper level art class? All the students would salivate over you."

"Aren't those done naked?" Jaden asked. "Not really my thing."

"Then maybe I should tie you to my bed and ride you whenever I feel like it," Maddie said, running a hand down to his stiffened cock and lightly squeezing it.

"That's what I'm talking about." He groaned. "I need to be inside you again."

"Ready when you are," she said, lifting one leg up over his hip. He held it, and she jumped to loop her arms around his neck, him catching her by her other thigh.

A change in the angle of her hips and she was able to slide down his length with ease, the way he was holding her wide open making their joining deeper than ever.

"Jaden!" she gasped, and then shrieked a little as he walked her under the cold spray of the shower.

"I told you I'd try for warm," he said with a smirk. "Don't worry, you won't even notice in a minute."

"You'd better be right," Maddie muttered. Her back hit the tile wall and she forgot what they were talking about in two short thrusts of his hips. He'd turned her into some kind of sex monster. She couldn't believe how free she felt in his arms.

"Oh yeah, babe, this will do it for me quick," Jaden panted in her ear. "How's the angle for you?"

"I really can't complain," Maddie gasped. She was practically folded in half, her knees up by her chest. His cock was dragging against a spot inside her that was simultaneously so deep and so pleasurable that she felt like she was flying and drowning all at once.

"Maddie, babe, I'm going to come," Jaden warned.

"Just keep going!" she begged. "So close!"

"Fuck, you're so sexy," Jaden bit out. "Come on."

He shifted infinitesimally within her and she broke apart, crying out, the pleasure almost too much to bear. He kept his hips moving even as he pumped within her, her walls milking his cock for every last drop he had.

"Oh my god," Maddie groaned, her body twitching with aftershocks.

"I'll say."

They discovered that the water did, in fact, warm up. It just took a while.

After they were dressed again, Jaden led her through the tunnels to the fighter's entrance. "Thanks for dropping by, babe," he said, giving her a prolonged kiss against the outside wall. "I'm going to go get my workout in."

"Didn't you already do that?" she teased.

"I missed some muscle groups," Jaden replied with a chuckle.

"Well, now we know what we need to work on for next time."

"Yeah." Jaden kissed her one last time and vanished back through the doors.

Maddie leaned against the wall for a minute, trying to get her bearings. She felt thoroughly wrung out, still throbbing between her legs despite having lost count of the number of times she'd orgasmed.

A thought occurred to her then and she rolled her eyes.

Damn it!

We didn't talk first!

She turned to the doors, but hesitated, fingers on the handle. "I don't think interrupting his workout is such a good idea."

She pulled her phone out and texted Chloe, asking for Hera's number.

"She'll know where the brothers live.

I'll thank her for bringing Arachne to make the clothes, too," she muttered to herself as she started walking home. "They might not have worked the way *I* intended them to, but at least I know that Jaden's really into me. I'm not just a one night stand." She sighed deeply. "I hope."

CHAPTER EIGHT

JADEN LET THE weights down carefully from his back press, barely making a *clink* as they touched the single weight left on the platform. His muscles felt good, a slight burning that told him he'd worked hard, but not worn himself out completely.

He wandered over to the open floor space. There were tractor wheels resting against the wall at the side, but he wasn't interested in them today. Instead, he lowered himself onto a mat and started his cool down stretches, starting with the large muscle groups and working down to the smaller ones.

At last, he heaved himself to his feet, muscles feeling loose and floppy, and made his way back to his ready room.

It still smelled like sex and Maddie's perfume.

Jaden groaned, his cock jumping to attention in an instant and making him dizzy at the redirection of blood flow.

"She's not here," he hissed at it, feeling more than a little ridiculous. He yanked out some paper towels and wet them, squatting by the table, where the first mess of spunk was pooled. He scrubbed at it vigorously until it was gone, and then moved on to the spot in front of the shower.

After cleaning, his hard-on hadn't diminished in the slightest, so Jaden got into the shower and crossed his fingers that the warm water would work again.

It didn't.

He cursed it, and then his *still not flagging* arousal.

"Fucking hell," he muttered, grabbing the soap and lathering it up between his palms. The sensation of touch combined with the suds against his body made him shudder and he rolled his eyes at his body's weakness.

"Fine. You want to come? Again? Go right ahead," he told himself, taking his cock in hand. "It's only been an hour since you came twice, but sure, why not? It'll be a pathetic showing, hardly any juice at all, but have it your way," he continued, berating himself as he stroked his hand up and down his shaft. In reality, he was already close and wanted to scream because it felt so good.

In an embarrassingly short time, Jaden's body succumbed to pleasure, the milky white fluid shooting from him and swirling down the drain between his toes. He braced himself on the wall, legs trembling.

"You're ridiculous," he told himself. "You just saw her."

Jaden straightened and finished with his shower, drying off and getting ready to head home. He glanced around the little room, making sure it was clean for Augustine, who would be using it tomorrow. He shuffled closer to the door as he was locking it, letting a cluster of people pass by him in the narrow hallway.

A sharp prick in the side of his neck, and his legs felt like jelly.

"I've got ya bud," snarled a voice in his ear, and then blackness closed in and Jaden knew no more.

***

Jaden woke up with a start, gasping for air and dripping wet. He tried to wipe his face and found his arms tied behind his back to a metal folding chair.

Cruel chuckles filled the air.

"Nice to see our *guest* is awake," snarled one man.

Deciding it would be useless to pretend to still be unconscious, Jaden blinked his eyes furiously to remove the last of the water droplets. His mouth felt like cotton and his head was spinning slightly from whatever drug they'd pumped into him.

There were three men in the room with him. He ignored them for a moment, looking around at his accommodations. The walls were cement, no windows. There were exposed pipes on the ceiling, and a single fluorescent light in the center, hanging precariously from wires. One wall had a crack halfway up the foundation; both it and the floor were slightly discolored from water seeping through it.

Definitely a basement then.

He wrinkled his nose in disgust as the stench of rot and the ozone tang of metal and cement hit him.

The largest man in the room gripped Jaden's chin, turning him back to facing the front. "I asked you a question!" he snapped.

"Did you? I must still be a bit loopy from the drug," Jaden replied, shrugging his shoulders.

The man growled at him, his bushy black eyebrows snapping down over his beady eyes. Jaden saw the intent to punch him broadcast in the way the man's shoulders shifted and tensed under his shirt. He tried to shift into his dragon form, to bust out of the room, to thicken his skin, anything.

Nothing happened.

Well, other than the fist connecting with his face.

Then his body hitting the floor as the chair tipped over.

The two other men sniggered as the first one walked around the chair to

Jaden's head and crouched down, his polished shoes filling Jaden's vision. "Did that clear your head at all?" the man snarled.

Huh.

Whatever they gave me must be preventing my transformation.

What could do that?

Jaden ignored the man even though it would piss him off.

The shoes moved away and the man told his lackeys to pick Jaden up off the floor. One lackey was tall and wiry, the other short and developing a paunch. Once Jaden's chair was up on all four legs again, the first guy dragged a chair over and sat in it.

"I feel like we got off on the wrong foot," the man said. "My name's Typhon."

Jaden glared and spat out some blood on the floor far enough away he wouldn't be likely to fall into it. "Lovely to meet you," he sneered sarcastically. "Like what you've done with the place. Certainly makes it feel homey."

The tall man snickered quietly and Jaden heartened. Maybe he'd have an ally of some sort.

Typhon turned halfway around and the tall man stopped.

Or maybe not.

Jaden rolled his eyes.

Lackeys was the right word for them.

"Do they follow you everywhere?" he asked, wanting to see if their loyalty was as unwavering as their leader seemed to think it was.

"Sure." Typhon shrugged.

"Poor sods. They wipe for you, too?"

The lackeys growled and Typhon raised a hand to quiet them, appraising Jaden with his eyebrows raised. "You're in no position to make me angry."

"On the contrary, I think I'm doing just fine."

Typhon crossed his arms and leaned back in his chair. "Leave us," he said.

Jaden smirked. He'd gotten under the guy's skin and Typhon was clearly worried about potential lasting impacts. Choosing to dismiss his lackeys just proved he wasn't as strong as he pretended to be.

Once the heavy door closed behind them, Typhon braced his arms on his knees, an ugly sneer on his face. "We're going to have a chat, you and me. I'm only going to say this once, so listen closely. You leave Ruby alone."

Who's Ruby?

Jaden's expression didn't change with his internal confusion. "Women are capable of making their own decisions."

"The fuck they are!" Typhon snarled. "I claimed her when we entered Valhalla's Throne tonight. You had no fucking right to her."

Seriously?

I can't believe this guy.

Jaden spat out more blood. "She has the right to her own body. No man can claim her, me included."

Typhon leapt to his feet and paced the length of the room.

Jaden was honestly surprised at the turn of events.

Have I been kidnapped and held hostage because I somehow made a move on this guy's girl?

MEDUSA

The only girl I've even talked to is...

He snickered out loud. "Did this 'Ruby' have red hair?"

"Of course she did! Why else would she have that name?" Typhon snarled.

"I think there might have been a misunderstanding. The only woman I've been with is unattached," Jaden attempted to placate the man. "She came to see me tonight at work. You must have gotten her confused with your girl."

Typhon got up in his face, his breath stinking like piss-poor beer. "I met my Ruby at the door tonight. She was supposed to sit on my lap while we watched the fights, having a good time. But my men spotted her sitting somewhere else and then followed her. She went into *your* room backstage.

They said there was no mistaking the noises that followed." Typhon growled and pushed off the chair, rocking it backward and making Jaden throw his weight forward to avoid smashing his head on the concrete floor.

A cruel smirk played at Typhon's lips. "So either you fucked my girl, or you weren't in your room and someone else did."

Jaden's mind was racing.

Is it possible that Maddie is this guy's girl and she lied to me?

He frowned, not liking that possibility. But it also seemed unlikely.

Why would she come find me when her boyfriend was right there?

And then he remembered something else.

Chloe got pissed off when I mentioned

I'd had sex with Maddie.

Could it be because it was proof her friend was cheating?

Typhon had returned to the chair in front of him, one leg crossed over the other at the ankle. He had a smirk as if he had Jaden caught between a rock and a hard place.

Wait a minute!

I met Maddie at a singles speed dating event!

There's no way she'd be with this guy and go to that.

Finally, what Typhon had said sank in. "You met her tonight? For the first time?"

"What of it?" Typhon snarled. "The sparks flew. She was mine the instant I laid eyes on her."

"Wow. Women are not property. But if

they were, she'd be mine." Jaden grinned, showing all his teeth. Not quite as intimidating as when he was in dragon form, but he'd take what he could get. "I met her two weeks ago."

"I saw no mating bite. She didn't have your scent on her," Typhon exclaimed.

"You're a shifter?" Jaden asked. "And what makes you think I am?"

"I'm a dragon shifter. One of the first." Typhon sniffed the air around Jaden and spat in his face. "I know the scent of one of my kind, even if you're one of the lesser shifters, breeding with *mortals,*" he grimaced at the word. "How do you think I knew to lace the knockout drug with an inhibitor?"

Makes sense.

He'd known that there were other dragon shifters, obviously, but hadn't met any since he'd woken up.

"Are the other two shifters as well?" He nodded toward the door to indicate the lackeys.

Typhon sneered. "As if. No, those two are human. They don't know what we are, only that I exude power and I sometimes let them share in it."

"Good setup for you," Jaden said thoughtfully. "Like a mafia boss. What sort of things are you into?"

"Wouldn't you like to know," Typhon growled. "Well, you'll find out soon enough. Right now, we're discussing Ruby. I know where she lives. I'll deal with her after I deal with you."

The first twinge of fear tickled at Jaden's heart. He couldn't protect Maddie from inside a box. The only solace he took from that was that she was second. He couldn't break, because she'd be next. Pretending she meant nothing to him might actually save her life. Jaden stared up into Typhon's black eyes and cocked an eyebrow. "Deal with her all you like. I was getting bored anyway," he said and yawned. "Are you going to show me to my room? A five-star establishment like this probably has king-sized beds. My double back home was getting old."

Typhon punched him again, this time unexpectedly.

The chair skidded sideways before toppling over again, pinning Jaden to the ground.

Fuck that hurts.

Jaden checked his teeth with his tongue. One of the back molars felt a little loose and he mentally cursed

Typhon in every language he knew.

"Didn't I tell you not to piss me off?" Typhon growled, hauling him upright again. "You have *no idea* what I'm capable of." He walked over to the door and knocked on it twice. It opened immediately.

"Yes, Boss?" one of the lackeys asked.

Typhon muttered something too quietly for Jaden to hear, and then the door closed again.

"Arranging for my meal? I like my steak medium-rare, just a little bloody, you know?" Jaden said.

"Laugh all you like, little mutt. You'll be singing a different tune soon enough." Typhon seemed amused by the thought.

The door opened again, and a lackey came in with a thick syringe of clear liquid.

"A little drug of my own concoction," Typhon said with a grin. "It heightens *every* sensation. You'll love it."

"You're not really my type," Jaden bit out.

"Don't worry, you won't care about that once I get started." Typhon stuck the needle in Jaden's neck.

Jaden instantly felt the cool sensation of the liquid in the syringe working its way through his bloodstream. He could feel every molecule of air in the room, his clothing felt too restrictive and rough on his skin. His chest rose and fell with each breath he took, his heart pumping loudly in his ears.

He barely registered a thick chain being tossed over an even thicker beam in the ceiling. One of the lackeys was untying his wrists from the chair, and each shift of the thick rope and chains over his extra sensitive skin felt like sandpaper over an open wound.

Jaden gritted his teeth, refusing to give Typhon the satisfaction of knowing that he got to him.

His arms were hauled up backward, straining his sockets to the limit, the pain shooting right into the primordial part of his brain. Jaden stood in an awkward half-bent forward position, like he was bowing before royalty, sweating in pain.

"This looks comfortable," Typhon said jovially. "Why don't you bring in the food you've prepared for our guest? Make sure to put it at the appropriate distance."

A bowl of something steaming was brought in by the short man and placed on the chair in front of Jaden.

"Sleep well," Typhon said cheerfully, and all three men left the room, the door closing behind them with a thud.

The aroma of whatever it was taunted Jaden. He hadn't eaten anything after his fight because Maddie had surprised him in his room, and then they'd had sex multiple times, and *then* he'd worked out.

He was fucking *starving*.

But even with stretching beyond his limits, there was no way he could reach the bowl of food.

"Appropriate distance indeed," Jaden muttered to himself mockingly. "Sleep well. Jackass."

Jaden knew he wouldn't be getting any sleep that night.

CHAPTER NINE

MADDIE SPENT THE entire next day on edge, eager to see Jaden again.

Eager and nervous.

She was a little worried that going to his house would be like cornering a caged wild animal.

"See you tomorrow!" she called after Alexander, blowing the toddler kisses that the little boy returned.

With their last charge picked up, she

locked the front door with a sigh of relief and joined Hestia in the kitchen.

Maddie picked up the dishtowel and hip-checked Hestia out of the center of the sink. "So what's new with you?"

Hestia raised an eyebrow. "Nothing. What about you?"

Biting back a grin, but feeling the blush on her cheeks anyway, Maddie felt the overwhelming urge to giggle. "I think I met someone."

"You think?" Hestia chuckled. "Either you did or you didn't."

"Okay, I did." Maddie hugged herself. "I just don't know if he's as into me as I am into him."

"What's wrong with him? You're a catch!"

"Thanks, sweetie. I'm not sure if he's looking for someone to settle down with, or someone to have fun with." Maddie picked up a bowl and started to dry it.

"There's no reason that you can't have both," Hestia pointed out. "It would suck if you settled down with someone you couldn't have fun with."

"You know what I mean."

"I do. How many times have you seen this guy?"

"Twice."

"Who went looking for the other the second time?"

"Me."

"And what was his reaction?"

Maddie blushed.

Hestia grinned. "That good, huh?"

"Sooooo good," Maddie groaned. "I used to think I couldn't care less about sex."

"Wow."

"He's ruined me for all other men, I swear," Maddie complained. "Now I just have to get him to *talk* to me."

"Yeah, well. You know how men are about talking." Hestia rolled her eyes.

"Unfortunately." Maddie put the bowl away and picked up another. "I'm seriously willing to look past the emotional constipation if he could just keep giving me orgasms full-time."

Hestia looked shocked for a second before bursting into laughter. "You go get him, girl!"

"That's the plan." Maddie swallowed nervously. "Hopefully it works out."

"Sweetie, even if it doesn't, you'll survive."

"Harsh." Maddie put the second bowl away with a frown. "I don't want to just *survive*. I want to *live*."

Hestia splashed soapy water at her. "You know what I mean."

With a shriek, Maddie blocked more attacks with her dishtowel. "I should leave you to finish the dishes on your own!"

"You'd like that, wouldn't you?" Hestia teased. "Go off to your lover, leave me all alone..."

Maddie dropped the cloth on the counter. "All right. See you tomorrow!"

"Hey!" Hestia complained, water dripping from her hands onto the floor as she twisted around to face Maddie. "I was joking!"

"Nope. You said it." Maddie danced out of the kitchen and then poked her head back in. "You can go home early tomorrow, I promise."

"Go get your man," Hestia ordered, a

half-smile on her face.

Maddie grabbed her purse from her office, checked her phone for messages, and was out the door, locking it behind her. She didn't bother going home to change first, heading right on the street from the daycare to where Hera had said Jaden lived with his brothers.

They lived on the outskirts of the Underworld, which Hera had told her was great for the running trails through the woods nearby. The three brothers regularly ran there. The yards seemed to be larger than the ones closer to town, and Maddie found herself daydreaming about what she could put in a garden if she lived here.

Their house came into sight and she admired the white siding for a minute before opening the gate and walking up the pathway. Seeing no bell, she knocked on the red wooden door.

A very large man with blond hair ripped the door open with a *whoosh*. His gaze dropped from over her head down to her face, almost as if he'd been expecting someone much taller. He frowned.

"Hello," Maddie said nervously. "May I speak to Jaden, please?"

"I was hoping you were him. My name is Augustine. Will you come in?"

"Thank you." Maddie followed him into the living room. She sat on the leather sofa. "He isn't home?"

"No." Augustine sat in a chair opposite her and braced his chin in his hands. "He did not come home last night. We were hoping he went home with a girl, but he is usually back in the morning when that happens." Then he looked panicked. "Sorry. I did not mean to imply..."

Maddie waved her hand. "When was the last time he stayed out all night?"

"A couple weeks ago. He did not give us the name."

"That was me." Maddie smiled wryly. "At least, I assume so."

Augustine nodded, looking relieved. "It had been a while before that, so no doubt it was you. But it was not you last night?"

Maddie shook her head. "I saw him at Valhalla's Throne yesterday evening, but he was still there when I left."

"Then he would have come home." Augustine rubbed his jaw. "I have a fight in two hours. Would you like to come with me, see if you can find anything out?"

"That's a great idea." Maddie played with the end of her hair. "You wouldn't happen to know a way I can hide this, would you?"

Augustine smiled. "I have just the thing."

***

The walk to the fight club was silent. Maddie wasn't sure what to say to the giant man beside her. He would pause and sniff the air every once in a while. She didn't want to ask why. It seemed like a rude question to ask of someone she'd just met.

Instead, she fiddled with the ends of the black scarf Augustine had given her to hide her hair. She'd wrapped it around her head like a hijab. Hopefully, she wouldn't run into those same men again tonight. It was a different time of day, too, which might help as well.

Augustine led her through the back entrance, hesitating only when he got to the door of his ready room. "Can you find your way from here?"

"Why don't we see if his bag is still in there first?" she suggested.

"Good point."

Maddie held her breath, half hoping to see Jaden asleep in a chair, but the room was completely empty when Augustine unlocked the door. "Rats."

Augustine smiled grimly. "My sentiments exactly. See if you can find Odin. He has security cameras at the doors. Maybe they recorded which direction Jaden went when he left."

"I'll try." Maddie wondered what Odin

looked like, or where his office might be.

"He is hard to miss. Just look for the larger than life God with grey hair and a parcel of women trailing behind him." He chuckled at her shocked look. "His office is down the hall on the right.

"That'll help." Maddie resisted the urge to giggle. "Good luck with your fight tonight."

"I do not need luck," Augustine replied with a slight bow. "But I thank you."

Maddie wandered down the hall, hoping to spot the correct office. She was in luck. Not only that, but Odin was in his office. She knocked on the open door and smiled when the big man inside turned away from his computer.

"How can I help you, little lady?"

"One of your fighters, Jaden, didn't

return home yesterday. His brothers and I are worried about him." Maddie wrung her hands.

"You're not the cops."

It wasn't a question, but Maddie shook her head anyway. "We're not that concerned yet."

"And he was last seen here?" Odin turned back to his computer, fingers clicking away on the keyboard.

"Yes, sir."

A video of the back door popped up on screen, and Odin used the mouse to navigate through the reel. "When did he leave last night?" Odin mumbled to himself.

"He said he wanted to workout after his match yesterday," Maddie supplied helpfully.

Odin nodded acknowledgement and

skipped ahead. Several people left, their movements jerky in the fast-forwarded video. A cart pulled up to the door, and Maddie almost ignored it, assuming it was there to pick up the garbage, but then four people exited the building, one of whom was being dragged by two others. They deposited the dragged person in the cart, and then it pulled away, the three men following it.

"That was him!" Maddie exclaimed. "Who were those men?"

Odin paused the video and rewound. Right after Jaden had been put in the cart, the largest man looked right at the security camera with a smirk.

"It's like he knew we would find this," Maddie hissed. "Do you recognize him?"

"I do." Odin nodded slowly, rubbing his jaw with one hand. "He's a very dangerous man."

"All the more reason to get Jaden away from him!" Maddie exclaimed. "Where can I find him?"

"I don't think you should go alone…" Odin said hesitantly.

"I am more than capable of taking care of myself," Maddie said vehemently. "Why is this guy dangerous?"

"He's one of the oldest dragon shifters in the Underworld," Odin replied cautiously. "He's very strong, very fast, and very well connected."

"Not *that* well connected," Maddie scoffed. "I look after the child of the Lord of Purgatory."

Odin chuckled. "Try telling *him* that."

"Maybe I will." Maddie scowled. "Is he here tonight?"

A couple mouse clicks and the screen

changed to a view of the interior of the amphitheater. Odin leaned forward to scan the seats. "Yup, he's in the center block. He usually shows up for the McKellen brothers' fights."

"Only them?" Maddie frowned. "Why?"

Odin shrugged. "Maybe he's a fan."

"A fan who took things a little too far by kidnapping one of them." Maddie turned to leave. "Thank you for showing me all this. I'm going to go talk to him."

"Be careful," Odin said.

"Don't worry. What can he do to me in public?" Maddie asked with a chuckle as she left.

She decided to find a seat behind the men, to try to overhear what they were saying before she confronted them directly. Since Odin had warned her about these men, she thought it might be a good idea to be cautious on her part.

She squeezed past a pair of giggly women who had obviously visited the bar before coming here and sat a couple seats away, leaning forward as if she were riveted on the fight happening on the stage.

She strained her ears, trying to hear what the two men closest to her were saying, but it was futile over the loud fight and even louder audience.

Maddie sat back and huffed, crossing her legs and twitching her foot impatiently. She half-heartedly watched the fight, two buff women facing off against each other. They were circling each other, little swirls of sand kicked up by their feet, as they looked for an opening.

I don't get what's so fascinating about this.

The women charged each other, shoulders hitting with a loud *crunch* that Maddie felt in her clenched jaw. She winced, watching as they pushed each other, slipping in the sand, until one woman fell to her knees and the other did an impressive looking grapple that had the first flat on the ground in seconds.

The amphitheater burst into applause and cheers, and the women got to their feet to bow and exit the stage.

In the momentary quiet, Maddie heard a low voice say, "McKellen's up next. Do you have the—"

She didn't hear the rest because her heart had frozen in place. That voice...

That was the man who had grabbed her ass the night before! And it was coming from the big man in front of her and to the right... The one that Odin had said was dangerous!

Of course it's the same guy.

Maddie groaned.

Why couldn't things be easy?

Just like that, hearing the voice of that man changed her plan. There was no way she was going to approach him directly now. She was even more relieved she had thought to cover her hair.

Augustine was fighting on the stage now. He had a completely different persona on stage, Maddie was interested to see. Different from Jaden, too. Augustine was calling out insults to his opponent to make them lose their cool, but not just any insults; fancy ones that sounded almost Shakespearean.

Maddie bit back a giggle, not wanting to draw attention to herself.

I guess it's not too out of character.

I wonder if Hera knows he does this.

She found herself getting more into this fight compared to the last one and assumed it was because she knew one of the fighters. When it drew to a close and the fighters were bowing, the short man in the row ahead of her leaned over the skinny tall one.

She heard the short man say in a whiny tone, "Typhon, I've analyzed the McKellen brothers' fights. They don't make sense."

The big man, the one she was scared of, replied, "Hush. Not here. Come on." All three men got up and left via the main exit.

Maddie hurried after them, trying both to keep to the shadows and not look like she was following them. Fortunately, they were well ahead of her in the hallway. Their voices were quiet, but she caught a couple mumbles.

"—doesn't make sense—"

"—strong or weak—"

"—too random—"

"—trying to say?" That was Typhon. He had paused to stare at his shorter companion and Maddie ducked into a hallway. Typhon sounded like he was about to explode.

"—saying that they randomly throw fights on purpose," the small man whined.

There was a loud growl and then a thud. Maddie shuddered in her hallway, terrified to peek out to see what had made that noise.

"—back to the house," Typhon said. "Our guest will—"

Maddie's blood ran cold. They could only mean Jaden. There was no time to reach Chloe and get help. She'd have to trail them on her own. She swallowed hard.

I have no idea how to do this.

The voices in the hall got quieter as the men walked away. Maddie risked a glance and saw that they were almost at the door of the club. She waited until they'd left before hurrying down the hall after them. She passed a fist-sized hole in the wall and cringed. Typhon must be really strong to make a hole like that in solid concrete.

She nodded to the doorman, a Cyclops with one large brown eye in the middle of his forehead, and then paused before passing through the door. "Do you know how to get messages to the fighters quickly?"

"Yes, ma'am," the Cyclops replied, gesturing over his shoulder where a black phone was concealed in a hole in the wall.

"Can you let Augustine McKellen know that I'm following a lead, please?" She didn't wait for the Cyclops to answer before she was out the door and taking the steps outside two at a time, frantically looking both directions to try to find the three men.

They were walking quickly, nearing the end of the street furthest from the core of the Underworld.

Maddie kept to the shadows as much as she could, staying close to the sides of the buildings. It got easier when the storefronts changed to houses, as there were no neon lights illuminating her position.

The men turned a corner and she ran as fast as she could, glad that she was in good shape. When she got to the last house before the turn, she slowed and peered around the brick side, just in case the men were waiting for her.

She didn't have to worry. They were still ahead of her, turning into the walkway of a small house that looked like it had seen better days on the other side of the street. She waited until they were inside before crossing the street herself and slipping into the backyard of the house directly across from her position.

The plan was to cut through the

backyards of the next few houses to better sneak up on the house they had entered. She really wished she had backup.

As if in answer to her prayer, her phone buzzed against her leg and she pulled it out and answered it.

"Maddie?" Chloe's voice was a welcome relief. "Augustine just called and said you had a lead? Where are you?"

"About to do something very stupid. Hurry and stop me." Maddie gave her the address and then turned off her phone, continuing her way through the back gardens.

Hang on, Jaden.

I'm on my way.

CHAPTER TEN

DESPITE THE AWKWARD position of his body and the rumbling in his stomach, Jaden found himself dozing. He couldn't support his full weight on his arms, so any time his body started to sag, the pain in his shoulders would jerk him awake.

The food placed in front of him had stopped tormenting him about two hours after he'd been left alone. Either it no longer had a scent or his stomach had gotten used to the idea of not getting fed. He wasn't sure he wanted to know which.

Needless to say, he was awake when Typhon visited him in the morning. The tall lackey looked disappointed that he wouldn't get to use the bucket of water he'd brought in.

Typhon grinned. "How did you find your accommodations last night? Up to your standards?"

"Five stars," Jaden said sarcastically.

"Excellent." Typhon took another syringe from the shorter lackey. "It would have been more comfortable for you to take your medicine if you'd still been asleep, but where's the fun in that?"

Jaden tried not to react as the cool

fluid was injected into the thick muscle of his neck and he felt the heightened sensations of everything all over again. His shoulders, which had stopped aching at some point during the night, started again, the pain almost unbearable.

Typhon squinted at him. "You look like you need to take a piss."

He hadn't really thought about it, but now that it was brought up, his bladder felt unbearably full.

"You tell me one thing about Ruby I don't know, and I'll see about letting you piss in a cup instead of your pants." Typhon smirked.

"Geneva Convention says prisoners have to be treated humanely," Jaden gasped.

"But you're not human," Typhon

hissed. "And neither am I. Tell me where my Ruby lives."

"You told me last night you knew where she lives," Jaden replied. He'd spent most of his sleep-deprived night going over their conversation, trying to figure out a way out of this mess. "Even if I knew, you wouldn't hold up your end of the bargain."

Typhon roared and swung his right fist at Jaden's face.

The shock of the impact felt like he'd been hit by a truck, but Jaden was relieved by one thing; Maddie was safe for now. They didn't know where she lived; they couldn't get to her. He intended on keeping it that way. They could do whatever they wanted to him, he wouldn't tell them anything about her.

"You think you're so smart," Typhon growled. "You and your brothers. You three have cost me more money than all the other fighters combined."

Jaden thought about that piece of information for a moment. "You're gambling on the fights at Odin's?"

"No. That's illegal." Typhon smirked. "I help other people gamble."

"A bookie. Seriously?" Jaden rolled his eyes. "Could you get any more cliché?"

"How did Pollux beat you?" Typhon shouted an inch from Jaden's face.

Ears ringing, Jaden raised an eyebrow. "He got the upper hand. I was having an off day." He was prepared for the attack this time, a left hook into his ribs and then a right into the fleshy part of his stomach.

He worked his throat furiously to keep the contents of his stomach where they were. The stench of that mess would not be pleasant. "Here's the only thing you're going to get out of me," Jaden spat. He felt better about making a conscious choice to let his bladder go, rather than letting Typhon use it as a weapon over him. It would wash out.

The release was almost orgasmic in his heightened state, which he found more than a little disturbing.

It took a moment for Typhon to realize what was happening, before the smell of ammonia hit. His nostrils flared and his eyes flashed in anger. "You're going to wish you hadn't done that."

"Not a chance."

Typhon signaled to his lackeys to leave the room and followed them out. At the door, he paused and said, "By the time I'm done with you, you're going to wish you'd never been born."

"Fuck you!" Jaden shouted just as the door closed with a thud, leaving him alone again.

He had no way of tracking time in that room, no concept of day or night.

How long had it been since he was taken?

Were his brothers worried about him?

Were they looking for him?

Jaden had never felt so alone.

He was pretty sure the punch to his torso had broken something, or at the very least cracked a rib. His breathing didn't feel affected, so it hadn't punctured a lung. The bruising would be pretty bad no matter what. Jaden had seen the damage to Pollux, and now that

Typhon had brought him up, he was pretty sure he was responsible for Pollux's condition.

Okay, so they took me for two reasons.

They must have been planning to kidnap me all along, for losing my fight with Pollux.

A bookie, huh?

He must have had major odds for Pollux winning that fight and had to pay out big time.

So they had a drug prepared to incapacitate me and brought it along to knock me out.

They also had the sensation-booster, shifter inhibitor drug ready to go once I got here.

If I could transform, I'd be out of these chains in seconds and through that door like tissue paper.

Jaden amused himself with imagining that scenario for a few minutes before he remembered that Typhon was a diamond dragon. He shuddered. Those were some of the most ancient dragons. It had been rumored that the humans had wiped them all out, or so he and his brothers had heard once they woke up from their sleep.

Obviously not.

They had the knockout drug with them, so they were planning on kidnapping me anyway.

Then Maddie distracted me from my usual routine.

She also somehow got on their radar.

Jaden pictured Maddie from that night—the night before?—and swore. Of course, she'd been wearing that sheer top thing with no bra underneath. It made him feel feral that Typhon had tried to put his filthy hands on her. Maddie had managed to give them the slip and come to find him.

But now Typhon is obsessed with her, so much so that he was distracted from the real issue the last time he'd interrogated Jaden; the fight with Pollux.

Jaden smirked. If he could keep Typhon off balance, drop hints about a person that he wasn't asking about, even if they were fabricated, he might live long enough to be found. His brothers would find him if they knew he was missing.

He just had to buy them some time so they could realize he had been kidnapped and do something about it.

He drifted a little as he tried to come up with plausible hints about Maddie and the way the brothers fought.

It felt like many hours had passed before Typhon and his men returned to the room, almost a full day.

Maybe it had been night and they'd gone to sleep again?

Jaden didn't care. The more days that passed, the more likely he was to be found.

Typhon was smirking as he put a small blue object on the seat of the chair in front of Jaden. "Tell me about the dice," he said.

"Good luck charm," Jaden replied automatically.

Typhon punched him in the jaw. "Try again."

Jaden spat blood in the other dragon shifter's face. "If you know the answer, why don't you tell me?"

Typhon scowled. "We know that you and your brothers randomly choose what matches you lose. I assume you roll the dice before the match and only win if the number says so." He paused, looking at Jaden for agreement.

Jaden kept his face impassive, despite Typhon having guessed correctly. "Cool theory. That's just my good luck charm."

"Liar!" Typhon hissed, spittle hitting Jaden's face. He hit Jaden a couple more times, fists quick and punishing.

It took a moment for the spots to clear from Jaden's vision after that bout. He took careful breaths through his mouth; his nose was definitely broken. The hot blood flowed down his upper lip before dripping into a pattern on the floor.

Typhon wrenched Jaden's head painfully back by his hair. "How about you forget about the dice and listen to what we say. In turn, we won't beat you so badly that your brothers don't recognize your body."

"So, what, you want me to throw matches that you tell me to?" Jaden said, his voice a harsh rasp.

"Now you're getting it!" Typhon let go and Jaden relaxed with a tiny sigh of relief.

"Can I think about it?"

"You need to *think about it*?" Typhon ended in a scream. "What part of not getting beaten do you need to *think about*?"

"Well, you know, there's the part where I uphold my honor and dignity," Jaden said nonchalantly.

Typhon growled and moved closer. "You won't get those when you're dead."

"I wouldn't get them even if I signed a deal with you," Jaden replied. "And you won't get your precious 'Ruby' either way."

"What do you know about Ruby?" Typhon demanded. His eyes looked wild, unhinged.

Jaden bit the inside of his cheek to stop himself from smirking. This was almost fun, if he could ignore the pain radiating from his body. He counted himself lucky that Typhon hadn't remembered to give him another dose of the drug.

His gaze darted over the minions; their hands were both visible and empty. Since it was unlikely that they'd have a syringe in their pockets, Jaden relaxed a bit. He could worry about the drug if one of them left the room. "I know a lot of things about her," he said blithely.

"Tell me everything you know!" Typhon ordered.

"I know that Pollux has sloppy footwork and overreaches when he swings," Jaden said thoughtfully. "I should have been able to knock him down within a few minutes."

"So why didn't you?" Typhon took the bait.

Jaden scoffed. "That would make for a pretty boring fight, don't you think? People want to be entertained when they come to Valhalla's. I'm not going to take that experience away from them."

Typhon rolled his eyes. "Yeah, yeah, I get that. But why didn't you *win*?"

"I met 'Ruby' that night," Jaden said,

changing topics once again.

Typhon growled impatiently, his mouth opening to say something, but the large door swung open and distracted him.

A pure high note rang out and the two lackeys stopped moving, frozen in place.

"What the fu—" Typhon roared, heading for the door.

Around the metal door stepped the last person Jaden ever thought he'd see here, let alone again.

CHAPTER ELEVEN

MADDIE EXAMINED THE house from the shadows of its neighbor. The blinds were all drawn, but there was light coming from underneath one window in the back of the house. Heart pounding, she wondered how much time she had. Jaden had already been their captive for more than a day.

What could they have done to him in that time?

She shook her head, dispelling the intrusive thoughts. They wouldn't help her right now.

The light hadn't flickered at all since she'd started watching the window, meaning the men weren't walking around. They might be sitting, but that meant they weren't looking outside.

Heart pounding, she dashed across the unkempt grassy space between the two houses, coming up right underneath the back window. She pressed herself against the house, the red brick rough through the material of her t-shirt and against the back of her arms. Checking first for a basement window—none, thankfully—she grasped the edge of the windowsill. Bracing her feet on the brick, she pulled up until she could peek through the gap in the blinds.

The room was empty. It appeared to be a dining space, with a flimsy card table and folding chairs.

Maddie craned her neck, trying to see more of the room.

A sliver of kitchen off to the right.

There was no movement in any area of the house.

Dropping back down onto the grass, she wiped the brick dust from her fingers onto the seat of her jeans and crept to the back door.

She tried the knob first; it was locked.

Why would it be easy?

She grumbled to herself. Checking under the mat first, she found nothing but some creepy crawlies and old dirt. She reached up as high as she could and felt the frame along the top of the door. Something fell to her feet and she picked up a weather worn brass key. She slid it into the lock and it turned easily, opening on well-oiled hinges.

Thanking her luck, Maddie tiptoed into the kitchen, ears perked for any sound within the house. She tucked the key into her pocket, just in case she might need it, and closed the door as carefully as she'd opened it.

Maddie wet her dry lips with her tongue, preparing herself to use her gift. She wished she could take a drink of water, but didn't want to turn on the tap. Pipes could make such a noise when used.

A door to the basement in the corner of the kitchen was ajar, and the light was on.

The stairs were open to below, and Maddie swallowed hard, trying not to imagine what could happen if someone grabbed at her ankles between the risers. Lying flat on the kitchen floor and ignoring the grime, she army crawled toward the stairs, dropping her head down to peer upside down into the basement.

The result was slightly anticlimactic.

The entire space was empty. It was as if this house was only a temporary hideout. She wondered if the other rooms were as sparse as the dining room and basement.

The furnace and hot water tank were in one corner. All along the opposite wall, however, was a cement wall with a door near the bottom of the stairs.

Maddie frowned, pulling herself back up to a crouch. She hugged her knees to her chest as she chewed on her lower lip. If the men were up here and she went downstairs, they'd have her trapped. If the men were downstairs and she searched up here first, they might hear her footsteps.

The light being on in the basement helped her finally make the decision. She took the steep stairs one at a time, stepping as close to the edge as she could to avoid creaking.

At the bottom, she took a moment to calm her heartbeat and looked around to see if she'd missed anything.

She had.

Tucked under the stairs was a desk with a computer set up. On the screen was the view of the back of a man chained awkwardly to the ceiling. Facing him was the man the short one had called Typhon. The other two were against the far wall.

Maddie's heart broke at seeing Jaden on the screen. He looked awful. She wouldn't be able to look at him in person until she dealt with the other three or else she'd burst into tears. The edge of the door, she hoped, was visible on the edge of the screen, and she prepared herself to enter.

The door was heavier than she'd expected. She pushed as hard as she could, and managed to catch the two lackeys unprepared. They froze in place instantly at her high C, their bodies becoming like stone.

One against one.

She much preferred those odds, even if one of them was a dragon shifter.

"What the fu—" Typhon roared.

Maddie needed to put the table

between him and her before he caught her. She couldn't afford to have him choke her. She'd be defenseless.

"Maddie!" Jaden's voice was barely a croak. "Get away from him!"

Swallowing hard, she ignored him, focusing her entire attention on the dangerous man closing in on her.

Typhon turned an interesting shade of puce as he stared at her. "Ruby?" he said, sounding flabbergasted. "What are you doing here?"

"Followed you. You see, you kidnapped someone I care about very much. You're going to pay for that." She was grateful she managed to say all that without a quaver in her tone.

"He's a dragon!" Jaden whispered, voice cracking in his urgency. "Get out while you still can!"

"Neat trick. What you did to my men, Ruby. How'd you do it?" Typhon asked, moving slowly around the table. Maddie kept pace with him, keeping the furniture between them.

"Family trait," Maddie said. Her back was to Jaden now, which meant he wouldn't get hit by her voice.

Typhon was checking on his men, putting his fingers against their necks to check for a heartbeat. He shouted, "You killed them! They don't have a pulse!"

"Don't be ridiculous," Maddie scoffed. "They're just stone. Like you will be." With that, she sang the same high C as earlier.

Typhon laughed. "You think that will work on me? One of the oldest dragons in the world? I've survived more than you can fathom, little medusa." Typhon walked closer to Maddie, making her back up.

She stopped singing.

His gaze flicked toward Jaden behind her and an evil grin spread across his face. "I know how to break him. And I'm going to enjoy every minute of it."

Maddie pushed down her fear and tilted her chin up. "I really don't think you will."

"Your voice is powerless against me. Unless you've got another trick hiding up your sleeve, I'm going to have to disagree with you, Ruby." Typhon lifted one big hand as if to stroke her hair, walking into her personal space to do so.

Her mother had once told her that the older the person, the harder it would be for her gift to work. Proximity would help, as would an increase in pitch.

With her mother's words in mind, Maddie prepared herself as Typhon crept closer and closer.

"That's it, my beautiful Ruby. Give in to the chemistry between us," Typhon crooned. His hands crept around her body, making her feel trapped.

If this doesn't work, I'm in big trouble.

She opened her mouth and shrieked the highest note she could muster directly into Typhon's startled face.

He froze in place, starting from his head down to his toes. His body had shifted away from her, as if the distance could possibly help him, keep him from suffering the same fate as his lackeys.

Spoiler; it didn't help in the slightest.

Maddie wiggled out of Typhon's rigid grasp, not caring overmuch if she broke his fingers, but not wanting to find out if the blood would be stone as well.

At last, she faced Jaden, taking in his damaged and bruised body.

"Oh my god," she whimpered. "What did they do to you?"

Jaden smiled weakly. "What didn't they do? They dosed me up with a drug that inhibits my powers, so I couldn't break out or heal myself."

She circled around him to examine the chains. "Do you know where the key is?"

"Sorry, no."

"Don't you dare be sorry!" Maddie said furiously. "Okay, I see how to lower the chains. Then you can sit, at least. I'm going to call Chloe." She pushed a chair closer to Jaden and loosened the chains until they fell with a clattering smash to the cement floor.

Wearily, Jaden sank onto the chair. "Thanks," he rasped. "Do you have water?"

"There's water in the kitchen. Do you think you can make it up the stairs?" Maddie worried at her lower lip. "I can't exactly carry you..."

Jaden huffed a laugh. "I'll try. There's no way I'm staying in this room any longer than I have to."

With Maddie hovering, unsure how to help him, Jaden staggered to his feet again. "I'll carry the chain for you, so you have some slack, would that help?" she asked anxiously.

"Please."

Once out of the room, Maddie paused only to pull the door closed and drop the latch in place.

"I thought you said they were stone?"

Jaden asked, confused. "Why bother locking them in?"

"Only for a short time; a couple hours at most," Maddie said as they started up the stairs.

Jaden nodded. "That door won't hold Typhon once he transforms."

"It makes me feel better." Once in the kitchen, Maddie called Chloe and put her phone on speaker before filling a glass with water and helping Jaden to drink it slowly.

"Chloe!" Maddie cried when the detective answered. "I found Jaden! He's been beaten within an inch of his life, drugged up, and who knows what else. Please hurry. The perpetrators are here, but I'm not sure how long Typhon will remain in stasis."

"All right, we're almost there. How

many men?"

"Three. One is a dragon shifter. Very powerful."

"I'm familiar with Typhon, don't worry."

"We need your help unchaining Jaden. He's..." Maddie looked at the man sagging in one of the folding chairs. "He's in really bad shape," she whispered.

"Hang on. The cavalry's coming. Front or back door?"

"Back. I used the key I found above the lintel." She opened the door.

"Like some kind of James Bond," Chloe teased. "Good girl. It's not considered breaking in if you use a key."

"To be fair, I would have broken in if I hadn't found the key," Maddie said.

"As a detective, I'm going to pretend I

didn't hear that. As your friend, I'm very proud." There was a pause and the sound of boots hitting the ground. "We're here."

"I've got you." Maddie looked at Jaden in the dining room. "Chloe's coming in with some of her coworkers."

Jaden grunted and swayed a little in his chair, which Maddie hoped meant he understood.

Chloe entered the house and gave Maddie a quick nod.

"Down in the basement," Maddie told her. "In the barred room. They're stone right now, but they'll be up soon. I don't know how soon for Typhon. I had to really push my limits."

"You are one badass bitch," Chloe said admiringly, pulling her into a tight hug. She ordered her people down the stairs quickly and headed for Jaden herself. It took her a matter of seconds to unlock the chains holding his wrists behind his back and he sagged forward.

"Jaden!" Maddie cried, running to support him.

Chloe checked him over. "He doesn't look good, Maddie."

"I *told* you that!" Maddie felt the tears thick at the back of her throat and fought them down. She'd be of no use to Jaden if she broke now.

"You did. It's another thing to see it for myself. I didn't think—" Chloe cut herself off. "He was such a smug asshole when I was interrogating him. So certain of himself and his abilities, sure that he'd never get hurt to a point that he couldn't heal."

"He mentioned being drugged,"

Maddie reminded her.

Chloe raised her eyebrows. "That might do it. Did you find any evidence of a drug?"

"Not down there. I haven't explored this floor yet. I called you as soon as we left the basement."

"Stay with him. There's no way he'd make it home on his own power. Call Hera. She can get a hold of his brothers." Chloe stretched her back with her hands on her hips before raising her wrist to her mouth. "Checking out the top floor. How are you doing down there?"

"Got them all bundled up and shifter-locked. Gonna sit tight until they wake up. They're too heavy to carry up the stairs," came the response.

Maddie shrugged and smiled

apologetically. "Well, they are like rock."

Chloe laughed. "So they seem to be." She headed for the hallway to the rest of the house, leaving Maddie alone with the semi-conscious Jaden.

"Hey," Jaden whispered. "I didn't imagine you?"

"Nope", she popped the 'p'. "I'm really here," Maddie replied.

"Thank fuck," he said. He blinked furiously, but a couple tears escaped. "Sorry you have to see me like this."

"You have nothing to be sorry for," Maddie said fiercely as she thumbed open her phone. "I'm going to get your brothers to come and get you. I don't think you can walk home on your own."

"They didn't give me another dose of that stuff tonight. It should wear off soon enough," Jaden said, putting one heavy hand on hers. "No need to bother them."

"They were worried about you. *I* was so worried." Maddie swallowed back her tears again.

"How long have I been here?" Jaden asked.

"You were taken last night, so about twenty-four hours," Maddie told him.

"Not so long, then," Jaden said with a half-smile of relief. "Time felt interminable in that room."

Maddie shuddered. "I bet."

Chloe came back just then. "Have you reached Hera yet?"

"He won't let me."

"Bullshit." Chloe glared at Jaden. "Let her." To them both, she showed a vial of clear fluid.

"I think this might be the drug that they used on him. There are crates of this stuff in one room, another is set up like a chemistry lab. What does it do?" she asked the question of Jaden.

"Inhibits powers, increases sensations. Pain, pleasure, everything." Jaden sounded exhausted.

"How many doses were you given?"

"Two, maybe three, I guess? I don't remember. It all blurred together. Do you have anything to eat?"

Chloe handed him a protein bar, which he gobbled and washed down with a gulp of water from the glass that Maddie refilled.

"Thanks. They didn't give me anything other than that drug and beatings."

"You're safe now," Maddie reassured him, running her hand gently through his black hair. It was matted with what she assumed was sweat and blood. She found the contact for Hera and dialed quickly.

"Hera, is Augustine with you? Can you reach him? I found Jaden and I need help getting him home." She gave Hera the address and hung up after her friend told her that Augustine would arrive soon.

"No, not *Augustine*," Jaden groaned. "He's been so smug lately." He tried to get to his feet and turned gray. A second later, he crumpled to the floor in a dead faint.

The two women stared at him.

"Well, that's one way to get out of seeing his brother," Chloe remarked dryly. "I guess we should make him more comfortable."

Maddie made a sound that fell

somewhere in between a laugh and a sob, something she didn't want to analyze overmuch, and helped Chloe straighten Jaden out. Running her hands along his ribs, she felt several that were broken. So were his jaw and nose. She could only imagine the colors that must be covering his skin.

A loud thump shook the house, and then there was a pounding on the front door.

Chloe pulled out her gun and approached the door carefully.

"Jaden? Chloe? Maddie? Let me in!"

"That's Augustine," Chloe said with relief. She put her gun away and unlocked the door for the big man.

He burst into the house, his presence immediately making the small room feel smaller. He whimpered deep in his throat when he saw his brother motionless on the floor. "Is he okay?"

"He'll be fine once the drug wears off," Chloe said. "Then his body can heal the usual way."

"We can't bring him to a hospital?" Maddie asked.

Augustine shook his head. "Not a good idea. His physiology would cause some problems."

Maddie frowned, confused. Jaden had mentioned powers, but not what they were.

What kind of supernatural being is he?

"He has a few broken bones," Chloe was saying. "How are you going to get him home?"

"I will fly him," Augustine said. He turned to Maddie. "Can you come along to make sure he does not fall off?"

"Sure?"

Augustine spotted a duffel at one side of the room and picked it up before Chloe could stop him, going through it.

"This belongs to Jaden. Can I take it?"

Chloe shrugged. "Go for it. Missing anything?"

"His lucky die. It is blue." Augustine passed the bag to Maddie and scooped up his brother, who protested even while unconscious. "Come on."

Once outside, Augustine slung Jaden on his back and transformed into a giant purple dragon.

Maddie blinked. It had been such a swift transformation that she'd almost missed it. She scaled the offered forepaw and got a good grip on both Jaden and

the dragon underneath them.
"I'm ready."

CHAPTER TWELVE

SHE WAS FLYING over Purgatory on the back of a dragon.

How many people got to say that?

Hera, probably.

She chuckled at the mental reminder.

She wasn't able to enjoy it much, however; keeping the unconscious Jaden from slipping off the slippery purple scales of his dragon brother required her full attention. Her hair ruffled in the wind, whipping across her face as they flew.

They landed in the street in front of the brothers' house so gently that she wasn't even jostled. The third brother, whom she didn't know, came running out of the house at their appearance, and helped Maddie get Jaden off the back of the purple dragon.

The instant she dismounted, Augustine returned to his human form, hurrying after the brown-haired brother to the house.

Maddie moved to follow them, but halted when Augustine turned to look at her.

"Can you get home safely?" he asked.

"Yes, but—"

Augustine cut her off. "He needs rest to eject the drug from his system and then recover from his injuries. You will not be able to help him."

She could feel tears filling her eyes. She wasn't sure if they were from anger or sadness. Probably a combination of the two.

The shifter bit his lip, anxiously looking over his shoulder at the house. "You should be able to come by after work tomorrow to check on him, if you wish to."

"Yes!" Maddie clapped a hand over her mouth after her outburst. Her nostrils caught the scent of dried blood on her skin and she fought back her gag reflex as she dropped her hand again. "I'll be here."

"He will be all right," Augustine said, putting a hand on her shoulder comfortingly. "Thanks to you."

Maddie walked home and hopped in the shower in a daze, mentally reeling from the exhaustion of the last hour.

Was it only an hour?

It felt interminable.

As quickly as her thoughts came, she felt awful for thinking them. Jaden was the one who had endured endless pain for what must have felt like days.

Then she felt guilty for comparing the situations. Just because he had been tortured didn't make her experience any less of a trauma.

She rested her forehead on the cool tile of her shower and let the hot water pour over her.

I told him I wanted to keep him in the corner of my room because he's pretty.

That has a totally different meaning now.

It was only when that uncomfortable thought occurred to her that she picked up the soap and scrubbed hard at the dried blood on her hands. The burgundy stains under her fingernails only served to remind her of Jaden's condition.

"He knows I'm not like those men," she reassured herself. "He came with me when I rescued him instead of cringing away from my touch."

She shut off the faucet and wrapped herself in towels. Her stomach rumbled, and Maddie suddenly remembered that she hadn't eaten since lunch.

"Oh bother," she muttered to herself, heading for the kitchen. "Well, it's not like I was exactly thinking about *food* before this."

Managing to make herself peanut butter on toast, Maddie barely tasted what she ate. After what felt like far too long, she toppled into bed, her hair still damp, where she spent a restless night.

***

Maddie went through her day at work in half a daze. One half of her mind was completely focused on her charges, keeping them safe and entertained. The other half, however, was running over the events of the previous evening. She couldn't understand why Jaden had been kidnapped. Typhon certainly hadn't seemed like a fan, not from the beatings that Jaden had suffered through. She wondered if Jaden knew, and if she'd ever find out.

As she'd promised, she let Hestia leave immediately after the kids had been picked up, and she had the daycare to herself while she tidied up.

Chloe had been the last to arrive, and she was able to reassure Maddie that the three men had been transferred into custody, with special protections on the cell that was holding Typhon.

"He transformed into a dragon while we were transporting him," Chloe confided quietly. "Nearly terrified my guys out of their wits! Thanks to you, though, we had enough warning. Even in dragon form, he couldn't break the special cuffs we had on him. He tried everything, but despite his form and size, he was no stronger than an average human. Thankfully."

"He was terrifying enough as a human. I can't imagine what he'd be like as a dragon," Maddie said with a shudder.

"Objectively, quite beautiful. I'd never seen a diamond dragon before," Chloe said. "Very sparkly."

Maddie giggled. "I'll trust you on that one."

"His cell is magically reinforced so that he can't transform and his strength won't be enough to break out," Chloe continued. "You can tell Jaden that he doesn't have to worry about them coming after him."

"Thank you." Maddie shuddered.

"How is he?"

"I haven't heard from Augustine, so I assume no change," Maddie said. "I'll know more once I get there this evening."

"Are you planning on staying the night?" Chloe waggled her eyebrows suggestively.

Maddie chuckled. "No, probably not. Well, not unless he's a thousand times better. But I'm not holding my breath."

"The McKellen brothers are tougher than they look," Chloe reassured her, picking up Atlanta. "Jaden will recover."

"Thanks." Maddie blew a kiss at the baby and waved to her friend as the pair slipped out the door.

As she washed the dishes, Maddie turned over what Chloe had said in her mind. Something was niggling at her, but she couldn't quite put her finger on it.

Finally, it hit her.

The McKellen *brothers*?

Augustine and Jaden looked nothing alike, and even though Jaden had said that he lived with his brothers, it hadn't really clicked...

If Augustine was a dragon shifter, did that mean that Jaden was too?

The possibility was mind-boggling. There weren't that many dragons left. It had practically been a genocide back in ancient times, millennia before she'd been born.

To discover that Typhon was one of the oldest dragon shifters alive was practically unheard of, and then to also find out that the McKellens were dragon shifters as well?

Her brain was too tired to be surprised.

"I'll ask Jaden when he's recovered," she decided, putting the last dish away. She dusted and swept the floor before grabbing her purse and locking up.

The weather was nice, and she enjoyed her walk over to the brothers' house. The third brother greeted her at the door, introducing himself as Finley. He showed her up to Jaden's room and asked her if she wanted anything.

"Just water, please?" Maddie asked, putting her purse next to the folding chair that was set up beside the bed.

Jaden had been bathed, blood no longer matting his dark hair or streaking down his face. His skin was still paler than usual, lacking the vitality that usually radiated from him.

"Has the drug left his system yet?" Maddie asked Finley anxiously when he brought her the glass of water.

"We think his body started to recover normally in the early morning," Finley said. "It's hard to tell. None of us have ever sustained injuries like this before. Even..." he trailed off.

"Thank you." Maddie lifted the glass and settled herself in the chair. It wasn't comfortable, but it wasn't meant to be. They wouldn't want to fall asleep when they were supposed to be keeping an eye on Jaden.

Finley left her alone, his heavy tread thumping down the stairs to the main floor.

Maddie reached out to Jaden's hand, fingers open and relaxed above the sheet, and traced the visible veins. She laced their fingers together lightly and searched his face for any sign of recognition.

His eyes shifted slightly under closed lids as he dreamt, chest rising and falling rhythmically in his sleep.

Maddie stroked the thin skin over his thumb and settled in for a long evening.

Hours later, she was startled out of a half-doze by fingers squeezing hers. Maddie's eyes flew open in surprise, meeting Jaden's hazel ones. "You're awake!" she gasped. She turned in her chair to call for his brothers, but he tugged on her hand.

"No," he said, his voice barely a whisper. "I'm still kidnapped, aren't I? You're a vision, an illusion, to help me get through the pain."

"No, Jaden," Maddie reassured him. "I'm really here. You're in your room at home. Augustine and Finley have been looking after you."

"That can't be right," Jaden said, turning his head away from her slightly. "I'm just the screw-up younger brother. I even screwed up with you. Walked away. I shouldn't have." His words were coming slowly, sounding slurred together.

He turned back to her, and Maddie could see that his pupils were large, swallowing up almost the whole eyeball. "It's all right, Jaden. You can rest. Heal," she suggested. "I'll be here when you wake up."

"No, you won't," Jaden said. A tear slipped out of the corner of his eye. "When I wake up, it'll be to more torture and pain. It's okay. This has been nice. It'll help me hold on a little longer."

"I'm really here with you," Maddie pleaded, hoping he'd hear the truth in her words. "Chloe captured Typhon and his men. You won't be hurt by them anymore."

"Why would you be here?"

"Because love is worth fighting for,"

she replied.

"Love?" he scoffed. "We've had sex a few times. But love?" He chuckled bitterly. "Not likely."

Maddie's eyes filled with tears and she dropped his hand. Wiping her cheeks, she got to her feet.

"Good to know," she choked out. "Goodbye, Jaden."

With that, she left the little room and stumbled down the stairs, barely able to see through the tears.

"Maddie?" asked one of the brothers from the living room, but she ignored him and pushed out the front door, running away from the little house as if she could leave her heartbreak behind with it.

CHAPTER THIRTEEN

JADEN BLINKED SLOWLY. Each time his eyelids opened, his pupils were a little smaller. Finally, he felt clear headed enough to sit up. He sniffed the air.

Maddie!

She had actually been there. He was in his own room at home, not the recreated version in his mind. His ribs ached from the awkward sitting position he was in and he sagged back onto the mattress.

Loud footsteps sounded on the stairs—*two at a time, must be Finley*—and then his doorway was filled by his brother Augustine.

"What are *you* doing here?" Jaden asked, too tired to add the usual bite to his tone.

"Maddie just exited the house in tears," Augustine snapped. "Pardon me for thinking the worst."

"I'm not dead yet," Jaden growled.

"What did you say to her?" Augustine demanded.

"None of your fucking business." Jaden turned his head away.

"That girl trailed your kidnappers from Valhalla's Throne, snuck into the house where you were held captive, and froze them like statues, all despite her terror of them. She saved your ass and you sent her away in tears? That made it my business."

Jaden was surprised to see how earnest Augustine was about this. "She got fucking confused with love," he said dismissively. "Hardly my fault."

Augustine snorted. "As if you hadn't been pining over her these past couple weeks. Wake up, brother, if you are not in love with her, you will be soon."

"Stop looking at everything through your rose-colored glasses," Jaden sneered. "I'm not in love with a girl I hooked up with twice."

Augustine raised an eyebrow.

"Your behavior has been different with this girl than with others in the past. For one, you have not bragged about your conquest even once. Two, you have stopped talking mid-sentence to daydream with a sappy smile on your face. Three, you called out for her multiple times during your sleep."

Jaden's jaw dropped. "I didn't."

"You did." Augustine sat in the chair and leaned close to his brother. "And you are going to fix this with that girl as soon as possible. I have her number—"

But Jaden had stopped listening to his brother.

Had he really called out for Maddie in his sleep?

It wouldn't surprise him.

Jaden thought about how he felt about her. How her energy, for lack of a better word, called to him deep within his soul.

"Holy shit, I love her," he said,

swinging his legs off the side of the bed.

"Where do you think you are going?" Augustine asked.

"I've got to tell her." Jaden pushed back the blankets and struggled to stand up. His ribs pinched and his lungs felt tight.

Augustine put a hand on Jaden's shoulder, the weight of it nearly causing his knees to buckle.

Jaden's ears were buzzing. He saw his brother's lips move, but the sound didn't register. He shrugged off the hand and took two stumbling steps to the doorway, catching himself on the frame.

More buzzing, and the hands were back, grabbing his wrist, trying to pull him and put him in bed.

He didn't want to go.

He had to get to Maddie.

He had to make this right.

Jaden had no idea how he got down the stairs, but he was at the bottom, hanging onto the post for support.

Finley was staring at him, arms crossed.

"Where do you think you're going?"

"Have... to... tell... Maddie..." Each word was a struggle to get out.

Definitely punctured a lung.

That'll be a bitch to heal.

"Dressed like that?" Finley raised an eyebrow.

Jaden hadn't noticed before, but he was completely naked.

Right, I wasn't exactly wearing clean clothing when I was strung up in chains, was I.

"Thanks for keeping my bed clean," he said, and the words were a little easier to get out.

Maybe going down the stairs took more out of me than I realized.

He pushed off the post and tried to squeeze by Finley, who didn't move an inch.

"There's nothing to lean against out there," Finley pointed out. "Are you going to crawl down the street to get to her?"

"More like fly," Jaden said, grinning. His skin rippled with green scales, and he gasped as a rush of energy accompanied them.

"Oh yeah. I'll catch you guys later." Already half-shifted, he pushed the rest of the way past Finley and out the front door.

Protests from his brothers rang in his ears as he fully transformed on the doorstep, taking a leap into the air before his wings had fully manifested. They caught him as he fell, unfurling and catching an updraft that made his stomach swoop with the exhilaration of flying. He scanned the neighborhood, squinting through the duskiness of the evening for Maddie's lone form.

She was quite a lot further along than he'd thought she would have gotten, her long legs covering the ground at a rapid pace.

Or it took me longer to get downstairs than I thought.

He chuckled to himself as his wings swept down, bringing him almost above her in one motion. He dropped into a controlled fall until he was hovering above her. Gently, he wrapped one hand around her waist, making her yelp with surprise.

"It's me," Jaden said, his voice echoing strangely from his dragon form. It had been a while since he talked while shifted.

Maddie stopped struggling the instant she heard his voice.

"Jaden? Shouldn't you be in bed?"

Jaden didn't reply. It was suddenly becoming more of a struggle to remain aloft, and he needed to concentrate all his efforts into his wings. He also wanted to be human when they had this conversation.

Thankfully there wasn't far to go, as a dragon flies, to get to Maddie's house. He landed unsteadily on her front lawn, put her down, and crumpled, all the energy leaving his muscles. He felt his loss of control over his shift.

"Shit," he muttered, face smushed

into the grass.

Not the most romantic method of telling someone you love them.

Darkness invaded his vision. And then he knew no more.

CHAPTER FOURTEEN

MADDIE STAYED ON her hands and knees on her lawn for a few moments, trying to catch her breath. She'd just been scooped up and carried by a dragon.

Yeah, okay, she'd ridden Augustine the night before. But this was different.

For one thing, she had *expected* the ride on Augustine.

For another, she'd been on his back,

not being held in a strong claw.

To give Jaden credit, he hadn't hurt her. She was out of breath from the suddenness of it all, not from being squeezed too tightly.

"Why are you here, Jaden?" she asked shakily, still facing away from him. She rolled into a sitting position, facing him. She was surprised by herself, her ability to face the man who had essentially told her she was a fling and broken her heart. Maybe it was the surprise of seeing him so soon. Maybe it was because he was a gigantic green dragon.

"Shouldn't you be recovering in bed?"

Something about the dragon didn't look quite right.

"Jaden?"

"Shit," he cursed, and then the

dragon vanished completely, leaving a completely naked and unconscious man on her front lawn.

Maddie's jaw dropped open.

"Jaden!" she gasped. He didn't look good. She crawled over to him, putting her fingers against his neck. It took her a moment to find it, but he had a thready pulse. Fumbling in her purse, she yanked out her phone and dialed Hera, putting the phone on speaker.

"Maddie? Everything all right?"

"No! Jaden collapsed and his pulse is weak and I don't know what to do!"

"Put Augustine on the line," Hera said, her tone shifting into business mode.

"I can't!" Maddie wailed. "We're in front of my house."

"That's a story I look forward to

hearing. Be there in a tick."

The line died and Maddie stared at it.

"How long is a tick?" she asked it desperately.

"About two breaths," Hera said from behind her. She knelt on the other side of Jaden and examined him quickly. "I've got just the thing," she said at last, pulling a vial from a satchel around her waist. "Help me sit him up."

Working together, the two women managed to roll him onto his back and then prop him against Maddie's body, his head falling back on her shoulder.

Maddie braced herself on one arm, his weight hard to bear, and wrapped one arm around his waist to keep him from rolling off.

"Good. You're a natural," Hera said with a small smile. Deftly, she uncorked the vial and opened his mouth, dripping two to three drops in at a time and closing his mouth in between each set.

"Is he going to be okay?" Maddie asked anxiously. She couldn't see Jaden's face from her position. "What are you giving him?"

"He's going to be fine. As for what's in this..." Hera smiled mysteriously. "It's one of my rarest potions. I concocted it for Augustine and his brothers in case one of them ever got seriously hurt. It is geared specifically for dragon shifter physiology."

"That's amazing," Maddie said sincerely. "Why didn't they call for you last night when they brought Jaden home?"

Hera rolled her eyes.

"Believe me, Augustine will be

hearing from me about that. Trying to take care of things all by themselves." She muttered under her breath for a moment as she dribbled more of her potion into Jaden's open mouth. "They probably thought that his body could heal itself on its own."

"Maybe if he stayed in bed," Maddie said, rolling her eyes. "And didn't overexert himself, shifting into his dragon form."

"He really is the worst patient." Hera chuckled.

Jaden groaned, his eyelids fluttering.

"What..." He tried to sit up straighter and gasped, grabbing at his ribs.

"Stop that," Hera chided him, batting his hand away. "Now that you're awake, you can drink the rest of this." She gave him the vial.

Jaden downed it in a gulp and then winced.

"That tastes like black licorice. Disgusting."

"I'm sorry that my healing potion tastes terrible. I could let your lung continue to be punctured and your ribs continue to be broken if you'd prefer," Hera said, a wry twist to her mouth.

"Thank you," Jaden replied, abashed.

"You're going to need to sleep for a bit after this," Hera told him. "Why don't we get you inside? And under no circumstances are you allowed to shift for twenty-four hours."

"Yes, Doc," Jaden said meekly.

"I'm not a doctor and you know it, cheeky boy," Hera said, getting to her feet.

Together, the three of them managed

to get Jaden onto his feet. It scared Maddie to feel how weak he was. It was unnatural for someone who normally brimmed with vitality to shake with fatigue after only a couple steps.

She unlocked her front door and the women helped Jaden into the living room, where he collapsed onto the couch.

"I'll get you a blanket," she said, taking the stairs up to the second floor two at a time to her linen closet. She grabbed a pillow and pillowcase as well as the blanket and trotted back down the stairs with her load.

"He's out like a light." Hera met her at the door. She pressed a finger to her lips and chuckled softly.

Maddie peeked into the living room to see him curled up on her couch, looking entirely too large for it. "Will he be all right tomorrow?"

"The medication should help him sleep for about four hours, after which he should be fully healed," Hera said. "I'm not one hundred percent sure because I haven't tested this potion yet. It's safe to use, of course. He's just the first test subject."

"Gotcha." Maddie nodded her understanding. "Thank you so much for coming."

"Of course. Us McKellen girls have to stick together." Hera hugged her around the linens.

Maddie bashfully hid her smile at that, even as her stomach flipped uncomfortably. Jaden had all but called her a fling.

Was she a McKellen girl?

"Please let Augustine know Jaden's here and sleeping. They can bring him some clothing and collect him in the morning."

"They're probably worried." Hera smiled in understanding. "I'll go in person to tell him."

"Thank you."

After Hera left, Maddie covered Jaden's nude body with the blanket and stuffed the pillow into its case. There was no way that she could get it under his head, so she left it nearby where he could reach it.

She made a quick sandwich and then got ready for bed before settling on the couch beside his.

His face was relaxed in sleep, smoothing out the harsh lines of tension around his eyes and mouth.

Jaden is so beautiful.

Maddie found herself mesmerized by the deep, even breaths he was taking, the blanket rising and falling with the motion of his rib cage expanding. The bruises that had been so stark against the skin of his chest were fading quickly, already a pale green, almost yellow. It made her blood boil to think about how he'd gotten those bruises; they were fist-sized, and she knew the fighter he'd faced in the ring the night he'd been taken hadn't made them.

At least he has his powers back.

And then it finally fully hit her; Jaden was a dragon shifter!

She'd been raised on fairy tales where the dragon shifters were the villains. Obviously based somewhat on Typhon and his ilk, rather than the gentle, caring McKellen brothers. She wondered why there weren't more stories about what they'd been up to. And then she wondered if *they* were as old as Typhon claimed to be. Jaden didn't seem to be as jaded—she snickered to herself at the unintentional pun—as Typhon, and neither did Finley or Augustine, from what little she knew of them.

Her eyes drifted closed, lulled to sleep by Jaden's rhythmic breathing.

CHAPTER FIFTEEN

JADEN WOKE ABRUPTLY, all his senses on alert. He assessed his injuries; he seemed to be in no more pain.

A loud snore broke into his contemplation and he looked over at Maddie, sound asleep on the couch perpendicular to his own. Her body was twisted around and her mouth was open.

He chuckled, the snore not what he

was expecting from her. It was, however, what had woken him.

She shuffled around into a fetal position and her mouth closed, the snores stopping.

Jaden got to his feet and stretched, the blanket falling from his body to pool on the couch. He felt better than he had in days, and was feeling residual energy from the boost of healing he'd been dosed with. Quietly, he moved around the small house, first visiting the toilet and then entering the kitchen.

The illuminated clock on the stove told him it was three in the morning.

He poked around in the fridge, pulling out some leftover Chinese takeout and eating it cold. He hoped Maddie wouldn't mind. If she did, he could buy her the same meal again.

Wandering around her house in the early morning was like a flashback to their first night together, although this time, Jaden had no intention of leaving.

He returned to the living room and squatted down beside her on the couch. Her hair was falling over her face, and he tucked it behind her ear.

"Maddie," he whispered.

"Hmmm?" she murmured, not opening her eyes, but turning her head into his hand.

"You'll be more comfortable in your bed. Do you want me to carry you?"

"Carry?" she asked, her voice thick with sleep.

"I can carry you to bed," Jaden repeated, amused.

Maddie blinked slowly, her pupils focusing on him with difficulty. Abruptly, she sat up.

"What are you doing up? Are you feeling better?"

Jaden rocked backward on his heels to avoid their heads colliding.

"I'm feeling rested and much, *much* better. I've got a lot of pent-up energy that I need to burn, so I was going to go for a flight."

"No, you can't!" Maddie cried. "Hera said no shifting for twenty-four hours."

Jaden frowned. "Dammit. I forgot about that. I can't exactly go for a run dressed like this."

Maddie smirked. "I see no *dressing* involved." Her gaze skimmed over his body, almost burning like a brand, and Jaden had to take a breath as all the blood in his body rushed south.

Maddie noticed, and her grin

widened. "I might have a better idea more suited to your current attire, if you're up for it."

"I think we need to have a conversation before we do anything else," Jaden said. He sat on the couch he'd been sleeping on; if he stayed near her, he'd touch her, and then they wouldn't be *talking*.

Maddie sat up, rubbing her eyes. "What conversation?"

The words caught in Jaden's throat. He sucked in another breath.

"I'm sorry I made you feel like you weren't important to me. It has been a long time since I let anyone close to me. I... I was defensive and lashed out. You are... You are everything." He looked down at his hands, lacing the fingers together.

"When Typhon called you Ruby, claimed you as his, I wanted to rip his throat out. But more importantly, I wanted to protect you from him. What kept me sane was that he wouldn't go looking for you until he was finished with me. I don't know why I believed him when he said that, but I did. And I was right to. You were safe from him until you found me." He raised his head, meeting her sympathetic gaze.

"You saved me, even when you weren't there. Maddie, I love you so much that I'm terrified. I feel like my heart is outside my body; my heart is you."

"That was beautiful," Maddie said shakily. "Love you, too."

"Come here, babe," Jaden said, opening his arms, and she straddled his thighs, burrowing into his embrace. She shuddered and he pressed his lips to the top of her head. "What's on your mind?" he murmured into her hair.

"Why did they take you?" she whispered.

"Oh. Well..." he trailed off, embarrassed. "My brothers and I... We only lose fights on purpose."

"What?"

"We're really good at fighting." It wasn't a boast, just a fact. "And if we won all the time, it would be boring to watch." He ran the pad of his thumb over the top of her shoulder, feeling the soft skin and fragile bones underneath. "So, umm, we roll a dice. One in six chance that we lose the fight that day. Typhon is a bookie. And apparently he lost a lot of money on one of my fights recently."

"Oh no," Maddie breathed. "Is that why that poor man was beaten, the night we met?"

"Pollux. Yeah, poor sap." Jaden took a deep breath. "Typhon figured out that I threw the match. Wanted me to work with him, throw the matches he told me to. I refused. He... took offense."

Maddie snorted, burying her face in his chest.

Jaden hesitated and rubbed her shoulder again. "When a dragon shifter mates for life, he gives his mate a bite to mark her as his, warning off other predators. Can I give you my bite, Maddie?"

Maddie shivered in his hold. "It would protect me from bastards like Typhon?"

Jaden growled deep in his chest. "It

would act as a warning to men like him that you're not to be messed with unless they want to deal with me."

"And it's permanent? Like getting married?"

"Stronger than marriage. It's a permanent bond between us." He couldn't see her face and he wondered if he was going too far, too fast.

"Yes."

"Yes?"

Maddie sat up and he could see she was beaming with happiness. "Yes, I want to be bonded with you for life."

"Wow." Jaden felt a little dazed by her love and trust. "You're amazing."

"What do I need to do?" She tilted her head to the side and swept her hair out of the way. "Hold still?"

Jaden chuckled. "It works better if at

the height of ecstasy."

"Yours or mine?"

"Both. Think you can handle that?" Jaden smirked.

"I can't wait." Maddie rested her arms over his shoulders. "Does this mean we get to have sex now?"

Jaden leaned forward and pressed a feather-light kiss to her shoulder. "I was thinking more along the lines of making love."

"You are such a romantic!" she gasped, goosebumps spreading from the point of contact.

"Don't tell my brothers or I'll never hear the end of it," he mock-growled.

"Your secret's safe with me," Maddie replied, pressing their foreheads together. "What's the difference between having sex and making love?"

Jaden smirked at her. "Don't forget fucking. The difference is in the speed and intimacy, I think. When you visited me at work, that was fucking." Her breath caught each time he said the word, making him want to kiss her.

"When you brought me here that first night, that was having sex. We didn't know each other yet, so there wasn't as much intimacy. But now..." he trailed off as he gently traced the outline of her spaghetti straps, the skin under the pads of his fingers smooth and freckled. He dipped underneath the material, over the top of the swell of her breasts. He didn't understand how women's clothing managed it, but somehow this skimpy little tank top managed to give Maddie some amazing cleavage, even though her breasts barely made a handful each.

"Now?" Maddie prompted breathlessly.

It took Jaden a moment to remember what he'd been about to say, all his attention was focused on her. He tugged the material of her shirt down in the center, revealing her tight little nipples. A bit of a stretch, and the neckline slipped under her breasts, pushing them up and together. His mouth salivated.

"Now, I know you. I know how your body responds to my touch—" He pinched one nipple lightly, making her hips jolt. "And you know me. There are no secrets left between us. Everything is out in the open."

"I like that," Maddie replied, her eyes half-closed in anticipation.

"I know you do," Jaden said. He pulled her tighter, his arms spanning her back. "Love you," he murmured, a hair's breadth from her lips.

She moaned in response and swayed into his body, crushing her breasts against his bare chest.

Jaden captured her lips with his, sucking on her full bottom lip before licking into her mouth to dance their tongues together. He drew their kiss out, heightening the intensity until she was melting in his arms.

"Let's go upstairs," he whispered, pecking kisses over her reddened lips. "Can you walk?"

She scowled at him. "You might be good, but you're not *that* good."

Jaden chuckled and squeezed her ass. "Challenge accepted."

Maddie rolled her eyes as she got to her feet.

When she tried to adjust her tank top, Jaden stopped her with one hand.

"Leave it like this," he rasped.

"You have quite the kink for my boobs," Maddie teased him.

"I have a kink for you being half-undressed," Jaden agreed unapologetically. "It's super sexy. When you get to your room, get on the bed on your hands and knees and wait for me."

"Where are you going?" Maddie asked.

Jaden grinned. "If I tell you, it'll ruin the surprise."

"A hint?" she begged.

After thinking for a moment, Jaden said, "It's something that will cool things down a bit."

Maddie raised an eyebrow but remained quiet as she trotted up the stairs. Jaden watched her ass bounce with each step and grinned to himself before heading into her kitchen. He opened the freezer and grabbed an ice cube, popping it into his mouth. Moving to the cupboards, he searched through them until he found a small glass where he could place the ice when it became too cold for him or if he wanted to talk.

The sight that greeted him when he entered Maddie's bedroom almost made his jaw drop. Fortunately, he remembered the ice cube just in time and clenched his jaw shut. She was in the exact position he'd told her to get into, her breasts hanging prettily and her ass in the air. The shorts she was wearing were so tiny that he could see nearly everything.

Jaden spat the ice into the glass,

putting it on the bed out of the way, and ran his hands over her still mostly clothed rear.

"You are so beautiful," he rasped. "So hot." He hooked his fingers in the waistband of her shorts. "I'm going to help you cool off." Slowly, he pulled the shorts down until they were mid-thigh, revealing her glistening lips to him.

"Stay there for me, honey," he said, getting off the bed and picking up the glass again, sucking the ice back into his mouth. The frigid cube was sending strange signals to his brain, which didn't know what to do with itself. He was as hard as a rock, his cock practically weeping with desperation as he gazed at her desire for him.

"Are you going to just stand there?" Maddie squeaked. She attempted to look over her shoulder at him. "I'm feeling awfully exposed over here."

Jaden tucked the ice cube into his cheek. "Exactly how I want you to feel," he replied. "You were the one with the fantasy of making me stand in the corner to look pretty. Well, in my fantasies, you're dripping wet with anticipation, pussy red and swollen from my attentions but not able to come without permission. But first, you're going to pose like this for me because this is a view that I want ingrained in my memory into my next life."

Maddie shivered and let out a soft moan. Her head dropped forward.

He moved within reach of her, pressing his palm to her ass. "Are you willing to play my game? You won't come without my permission?"

"I'll do my best," she said breathlessly.

"Good girl," Jaden purred. "Move your knees back a bit, to the edge of the bed. No, not your hands. Put them back where they were. Feel that stretch?" The position stuck her ass up even higher and brought her head down onto the mattress.

"You can relax your head. Do you need a pillow or are you comfortable?"

"A pillow might help," Maddie admitted.

"Great." Jaden walked around the bed and grabbed her pillow, putting it underneath her head. "Comfy?"

"Yes."

"Thank you for telling me what you needed." Jaden grabbed her chair from the corner of the room and put it at the edge of the bed. When he was sitting in it, her pussy would be directly in front of him, ready for him to taste whenever he felt like it.

He held the ice between his teeth and blew around it directly onto her lower lips, making her yelp.

"Are you an ice dragon?"

"I'm not supposed to shift, remember?" he replied with a chuckle. "And no, I'm not." He spat the cube into the glass and ran the flat of his tongue over her folds, wiggling it between them to get at her clit and dip into her opening.

"Cold!" she gasped, rocking forward.

"Do I need to hold you still, or will you behave yourself?" Jaden growled.

Meekly, she returned to her former position.

Jaden tipped the glass to his lips, getting his tongue cold again. While he sucked on the sliver of ice, he pressed the glass to her pussy, amused by the smear her juices left behind on its side.

"Spread your legs, baby," he said.

Hampered by the elastic from her shorts around her thighs, she could only move them a little bit apart, but it was enough for him to slip the glass between them, nestled in the crotch of the garment.

He held the ice in his teeth again, this time pointed out like a tongue, and flicked it over the nub of her clit. Her shriek made him chuckle, but he relented and let the sliver drop into the glass, latching onto her with both tongue and lips. Her shouts turned to moans of pleasure that were music to his ears.

They grew higher in pitch as she got closer to her climax, and Jaden wondered if she'd remember her promise to not come.

He moved his mouth up slightly, leaving her clit behind to work his tongue inside of her body. Her inner walls fluttered around his tongue, and he lapped up her juices, groaning at her taste.

"Jaden, fuck, please, I'm not going to last much longer," she begged.

He could hear the desperation in her voice and smiled against her flesh, pleased with himself for having brought her there already.

"No," he said, and she whimpered as he moved back to her clit, scraping his teeth lightly over the skin of the hood.

"I can't—" she wailed. "It's too much!"

"No," Jaden ordered, returning to his feast.

Maddie's toes curled and her thighs shook. She turned her head into the pillow and muffled her scream, but Jaden could read her body by the fresh gush of fluid that flowed out of her.

"That felt like you didn't even try," he said, pretending to be disappointed in her. He removed the glass, putting it on her dresser. The ice had melted completely by this point. "You must want to come so very badly if you can't even wait for my permission. All right then. Instead of withholding orgasms, you must come every time I tell you to. Do you think you can handle following that instruction?"

Mouth agape, Maddie shook her head a little.

"No?" Jaden flipped her onto her back and she bounced a little on the bed. "What do you want then, babe? Tell me."

CHAPTER SIXTEEN

MADDIE STARED UP at her lover. She had never been so turned on in her life.

"I just want you," she whispered. She watched Jaden's throat work as he swallowed hard.

"I... All right, truth time. I've never *made love* to anyone before," he confided in a whisper. "What if I'm bad at it?"

She wanted to laugh, but he was so serious. Instead, she kicked her shorts off and held her arms out to him. He crawled over to her and she rolled them onto their sides. She ran her fingers through his hair in what she hoped was a soothing motion.

"Then we'll work on it together. Jaden, I love you. I'm in this forever."

Jaden took a deep, shuddering breath and buried his face in her hair. "Thanks. I needed to hear that, I think." His voice was slightly muffled and his breath tickled her scalp.

"Do you want to take a moment to talk? Cuddle like this?" Maddie asked.

"This is nice," Jaden murmured.

Maddie snuggled in closer, feeling the rasp of his chest hair against her still bared breasts and his leg hair against her inner thigh as she curled one leg over his. In this position, she felt very exposed, but not as much as when Jaden was eye level to her crotch at the foot of the bed, she supposed, flushing slightly. She reveled in the thrumming beat of his heart below her ear and chewed her lip.

"How old are you?" she asked as she trailed her fingers over the light dusting of hair on his chest.

Jaden chuckled, the vibrations from his chest echoing through to hers. "Thirty-four. Why do you ask?"

"Well, until recently, I hadn't heard about dragon shifters existing. And Typhon was millennia old. So I was just wondering..." she trailed off.

"Where I came from," Jaden finished for her. His fingers traced the top of her shirt across her shoulder blades. "I was born a long time ago, when there were many more dragon shifters. But we were feared by the humans, and hunted nearly to extinction. So Augustine, Finley, and I... We're not biologically brothers, in case you hadn't noticed—"

Maddie giggled. "You definitely don't look alike."

"We decided to try our luck with a witch. She was hard to find, and it was even harder to convince her that we were worth saving." Jaden squeezed her tighter against his body. "I'm still not sure how we did it. But after a year of doing her errands and helping her on her property, she agreed to put us into stasis. She promised that her spell would put us to sleep until the earth woke up. An added benefit to this spell was that nobody, not even herself, would know where we were resting."

"How did you end up waking up?" Maddie tilted her head back so she could see his face.

Jaden chuckled. "There was an earthquake, right under our resting place, a couple years ago. We got quite a bit of a shock when we left our hideout. Cars, cell phones, airplanes! Just... everything. We spent a lot of our time hiding, until we heard the rumors of the Underworld as being a safe place for supernatural beings. We came here, got jobs with Odin at Valhalla's Throne, and have been here ever since."

"Wow." Maddie kissed his collarbone. "I can't imagine how different everything must have been for you."

"I definitely prefer the houses. Mattresses especially," Jaden teased. "But the clothing back then had much easier access."

"I guess I can see that," Maddie said. "Sorry, but you'll have to pry my leggings out of my cold, dead hands."

"The clothing now does have its perks," Jaden continued, tracing the strap of her tank top over her shoulder from back to front and palming her breast. "Much more form-fitting and very revealing," he murmured, inching down the mattress to press kisses over her nipple. It pebbled and he sucked it into his mouth.

She clutched his head to her with one hand, reveling in the pressure he was creating. His teeth scraped over the bud and it felt like a direct current right to her clit. She writhed against him, catching her opening on the head of his cock. His length slipped easily through the residual juices of her previous orgasm, the head bumping into her clit as she ground against him.

"Naughty girl," Jaden said with a smirk, leaving her breast with the nipple peaked and reddened. He tweaked it between his thumb and forefinger and she gasped, hips twitching against him.

"Please," she whimpered, seeking his cock again. She succeeded in capturing his cock against her opening and rocked down, the thick head sliding inside her. She groaned and hooked her leg over his hip to spread herself wider to accommodate his girth. "Yes!"

Jaden pulled her closer by her thigh, thrusting up at the same time, and suddenly they were fully connected.

"Just... stay," she whispered, nuzzling their noses together. "Kiss me, breathe with me, be with me in this moment." She tilted her head to the side and pressed her lips to his, feeling the usual fuzziness that came from kissing Jaden. She hoped that would never fully go away.

His breath through his nose tickled her cheek. She could taste the evidence of her arousal on his tongue. His strong arms banded around her body, holding her to him tight enough that on each inhale, she could feel the rasp of his chest hair against her breasts. His thick cock was deep within her, twitching ever so slightly. She moaned, all her senses on high alert. Even the tips of her fingers as she ran them over the smooth skin of his shoulders were sending back pleasure signals to her brain. Her inner walls clenched involuntarily and Jaden groaned deep in his chest, the sound reverberating through her bones.

She broke the kiss with a gasp. "Want to be on top of you. That okay?"

"Yes," Jaden agreed without hesitation. He rolled onto his back, pulling her with him so that they remained joined together.

Maddie sat up, taking him impossibly deeper, and yanked her tank top over her head. It caught in her hair as she struggled to get it off.

"Babe," Jaden growled, "If you keep rocking on me like that, I won't be responsible for what I do next."

Finally free from the shirt, Maddie braced herself on his chest and smirked down at him.

"Rocking on you like what? Like this?" She bounced her hips a few times, forcing shallow repetitive thrusts.

"Fuck." Jaden's neck muscles showed the tension of his body. "Nope. Can't do it. Need to pound into you." He brought his knees up, knocking her forward onto his chest.

"Hey!" Maddie pouted. "I thought you said I could be on top?"

"You are." He thrust into her, snapping his hips up. "I'm just doing the work."

The breath knocked out of her, Maddie could only nod vigorously.

"Yeah, okay, this feels great. Keep going." The quick, sharp thrusts jostled her higher up his body. She braced herself on her arms, pushing back to meet him.

The heat was building between them, sweaty and glorious.

"Close!" she panted.

"Good. Come for me, darling."

A couple more thrusts, deep and even, and she shattered in his arms, a silent scream dying on her lips. She saw tiny sparkles of light behind her closed eyelids, the orgasm was so powerful.

"How was that?" Jaden slowed his movements while she recovered.

She melted over his body, no longer able to brace herself over him, a sappy smile on her face.

"Scrumptious," she murmured.

"That's a new one." Chuckling, Jaden rubbed a hand down her back, tracing the nubs on her spine with the tips of his fingers.

"I practically tasted colors and saw flavors. It was delicious," Maddie repeated. "Did you come?"

"Not yet. Sweetheart," Jaden rubbed her back again until she looked up at him. His face was serious. "Are you sure you want my mark?"

"Of course!" she replied, surprised. "I wouldn't have agreed if I didn't."

"I don't want you to feel pressured. It can wait, I promise."

Maddie cupped his cheek with one hand and ran her thumb over his cheekbone. "I'm not feeling pressured. I want your mark. Please."

Jaden turned his head to kiss her palm. "I needed to be sure." He sat them both up, the muscles of his abdomen tightening with the effort. "On all fours again."

"You've really got a thing for seeing me like that, don't you?" Maddie winced as she pulled off of him.

"It's really fucking hot, what can I say?" Jaden smacked her lightly on her ass. "If you could see what I see…"

"Describe it to me," Maddie said.

"Oh, baby, I love it when you talk dirty to me."

She felt the mattress rock as he shifted his position to get behind her, and then his knees on either side of her ankles.

"First, your ass. When you're standing up, you've got a bit of a pop of booty, but like this, your ass fills out and is so grabbable. Your waist dips in above your hips and there's just something about these three dimples at the base of your spine that is just so sexy." With each body part, he ran his fingers over her, demonstrating the place he was describing. "And then we get to your pretty little pussy. When you're on all fours, I can see everything from your clit to your taint."

Maddie jumped a little when his finger touched her clit. His digit slid through her juices until it ended up at the tight furl of her ass.

"Relax, baby," Jaden murmured, and she realized she was tensing against his possible intrusion. "If you don't want me to go here, just say the word."

She opened her mouth to tell him to stop when he circled around the puckered skin and slipped just inside. She gasped out a moan, her head dropping down to the bed between her arms.

"Oh my god! Is it supposed to feel that good?"

Jaden chuckled and kissed the small

of her back. "It can. Do you want me to show you?"

"Yes, please!" She couldn't believe she'd been shy about this two seconds ago.

"Your pussy opens up for me like a flower to the sun," Jaden continued with his description of what he was seeing as he slowly rocked his finger in a circle just inside her ass. "I can see your hot little cunt gaping open now that I've pounded into you. Dripping from it is your sweet nectar. I'm going to use that to stretch your ass open. Do you want me to fuck you in both holes?"

"You're... You're not supposed to transform!" Maddie managed to say.

Jaden paused in his movements. Then he laughed quietly and started again. "I meant using my fingers, love.

Or if you happen to have any dildos lying around.”

“Oh.” Maddie flushed a brilliant scarlet. “I’ve got one in my top drawer.”

“Kinky thing,” Jaden said affectionately. “We’ll see how well you stretch for me before I make any decisions, all right?”

“Okay.” He stretched her wider and she whimpered.

“You good?” He asked, concerned.

“Fine. What was that?”

“Second finger. You’re so tight. Gonna get some more lube for you.” Without moving the hand playing with her ass, he swiped his fingers through the wetness freely flowing from her vagina, and then rubbed it into her ass, coating his fingers there. “How’s that?”

“I liked the feeling of you in both

places," she confided, her blush not abating. "Made me feel full."

"I'm going to stuff you so full that you won't be able to move," Jaden told her, adding a third finger and stretching her further. "Just how big is this dildo of yours?"

"Not very. Smaller than you."

"You should be able to take it easily." He scissored his fingers and she moaned. "You're doing so well. Don't go anywhere." His weight left the mattress and she heard him open the drawer. "Right on top. Use this often?"

"Not often enough," she replied, making him huff a laugh.

"I'll make sure to use it often on you, how's that?" he asked, and his weight settled behind her again. "Oh, look at you. Still wide open for me. You want this?" He tapped the cool silicone against her pussy, a wet slapping sound echoing through the room.

She'd be embarrassed, but she was too turned on. "Yes!"

"Good girl." The silicone slipped into her pussy and she clenched down on it. "I'm going to fuck another orgasm from you with this toy. Get it good and wet, darling, and then it's going in your ass."

"Oh fuck. Please, touch my clit," Maddie begged.

"I love it when you use your words," Jaden said, immediately following her request.

Her body was humming with pleasure, walking the edge of orgasm as he played with her. Then his fingernail scraped over the hood of her clit and she shouted, falling into the abyss of sensation. She could hear him saying encouraging things behind her, feel him twist the dildo inside her, and then it was gone. Pressure at her ass, and then her body relaxed and it slid inside her, its passage eased by her own juices.

"That's it, I knew you could take it. Do you feel that? Does it feel good?" Jaden asked.

"So good. Jaden, I need you!" she whined.

"I'm not going anywhere."

The head of his cock felt so vastly different from the silicone of her toy. Different, and yet familiar now. He pushed inside her slowly, letting her get used to the idea of being so full from both holes. "You're even tighter now than you were," he said through gritted teeth.

Maddie gasped. "I want it. Jaden, fuck me!"

His body covered hers and he brushed her hair over one shoulder, exposing her neck. "Last chance. Are you sure—"

"Yes, I'm sure! Mark me as yours!" cried Maddie.

That seemed to do the trick. Jaden roared and started fucking into her so hard that she could feel it in her teeth. His breath was hot on her neck. He licked the muscle that joined her shoulder to her neck and then worried at it with his teeth.

She tensed a little, butterflies fluttering in her belly as the reality of what she was about to do sank in. Before Jaden could ask her for her consent again, she relaxed against his body with a moan.

His hand on her hip gripped her harder.

"Gonna come, baby. You feel so good, take me so well. Gonna make you mine. Maddie, my girl, my love," he grunted into her skin as he thrust wildly. "Fuck, yes!" he shouted, and then he bit down hard.

Maddie had expected the pain; he was biting her flesh, after all. What was surprising was the surge of pleasure that came with it. Her nerves took the sensation in her shoulder and fed it directly down into her clit, sparking the most intense orgasm of her life. The feedback loop built on itself until her brain couldn't cope with it and she lost consciousness.

****

When she woke up, she was wrapped in her sheet, her head resting on the firm muscle of Jaden's pectoral, sitting on his lap against the headboard of her bed.

"You're awake," he rumbled. "Are you okay? I'm so sorry."

"I'm not. I'm still tingling with aftershocks." She giggled.

"I didn't hurt you?" Jaden asked, petting her hair back from her face.

"That was incredible. I can't wait to do it again." She craned her neck, sitting up straighter to give him a kiss.

"You're not sore?" Jaden raised an eyebrow, his hand running down her body, pulling at the sheet to get between her legs.

"A little, but I ache to have you buried inside me again." Maddie spread her knees, giving him easier access. When his fingers entered her, her eyes rolled back at how good it felt. "Come on, Jaden, let's give your stamina a workout."

"Your wish is my command," Jaden growled, ripping the sheet off of her.

EPILOGUE

THE DAYCARE HAD colorful balloons and streamers around the front door. The decorations continued into the backyard, where the kid's talent show was going to be held. There was a table in the shade well stocked with sugary pastries from the ButterNut Bakery, and Hera and Augustine were already there, helping with the food.

Jaden went to find Maddie. She was

inside with the kids, who were bouncing off the walls with excitement.

"Is everyone ready?" Maddie asked them.

"Yes!" the ones who could talk replied.

"I think everyone's here now, so we'll all go outside to cheer for each other. Let's go!" Maddie cuddled Chloe's child while Hestia picked up a little girl that Jaden didn't know. The boys followed them outside, and they all sat on the grass.

"If I might have your attention, please?" Maddie stood in the center of the yard. "Your children have prepared a show of their recent achievements for your entertainment. First off, we have Shana. Come here, baby," she encouraged the little girl that Hestia had carried. She was sitting calmly in the grass, running her hands through it.

When Maddie called her name, she twisted around and started crawling toward her. Maddie greeted her with a big smile. "Good job, Shana! Lyta, are you ready to show your mommy and daddy your new skill?"

Lyta took Maddie's hands in her chubby fingers and helped the girl stand up. The little one wobbled before steadying. Then she took two steps forward.

A woman and man in the audience of parents started clapping loudly and Lyta fell onto her diaper-clad bum. Jaden chuckled.

"Thank you, Lyta!" Maddie cheered enthusiastically. "Now we're moving on to Damien and Alexander, who have choreographed an acrobatic routine for you."

The two little boys got to their feet and Maddie joined Jaden at the side of the mock stage. "They've been practicing this for weeks," she whispered to him.

He watched, impressed, as the boys did simultaneous somersaults in a mostly straight line. They got to their feet close to the parents, and then did cartwheels all the way back to where they had started. Finally, they did handstands. Alexander, the younger of the two, fell over first, but both boys were beaming as they took their bows.

Maddie ushered the boys back to the side as she took her place in the center again. "Last but not least, we have Atlanta! She's going to show off her shifting abilities!"

Jaden's eyebrows rose in surprise, and he looked at the placid six-month old sitting with Hestia. She had turned her head when Maddie said her name.

"Come here, Atlanta!" Maddie called.

The baby shifted into a wolf puppy with tiny black wings and trotted over to Maddie, her tail wagging proudly.

Jaden clapped loudly for her. Dragon shifters were much older than that when they first attempted shifting, as far as he knew. He'd been almost seven years old when he'd managed his first full shift.

"Thank you, everyone, for coming to our show. Please enjoy all the delicious treats from the ButterNut Bakery!" Maddie returned to his side and took his hand shyly. The kids were all chattering or babbling excitedly at their parents, who were beaming proud smiles at their offspring.

"Where's Alexander's father?" Jaden asked, pointing out the one solo parent with a child.

Maddie rolled her eyes. "Not in the picture. Artemis has been doing an excellent job of raising the boy on her own. He's such a darling, and much better off for his father not being present."

"That bad, huh?"

"He left when she told him she was pregnant." She glanced up at him. "How do you feel about kids?"

Jaden thought about that for a second. "I think I'd be a shitty father, but if they have you as a mother, I would do my best."

"Good to know." Maddie smiled and put her hand on her belly.

GINA KINCADE

"Wait, what!?"

Thank you for reading Medusa!

If you enjoyed this book, please return to the retailer and leave a review. Your words mean so much and help us to continue writing the books you love.

Follow our Facebook page
Speed Dating with the Denizens of the Underworld Series

Watch your favorite online retailer for the other books in the Speed Dating with the Denizens of the Underworld series.

EXCERPT

THE *CLICK-CLACK* OF Artemis Chase's four-inch spiked slingback heels echoed through the marble halls of Purgatory's only bank. The shuffle of sneakers followed, her assistant, Luna, right behind her.

"And Charon wants to open a branch on his flagship casino cruise ship. He's sent you a proposal."

"At least he knows how to do things properly," Artemis said. "Put the report on my desk and I'll look at the numbers this afternoon."

"Yes, Miss Chase."

"Any word from the jackass?" Artemis felt her stomach flip just thinking about the man.

"No, I still haven't been able to reach Mister Blanca," Luna replied apologetically. "I'll keep trying. There's still a couple weeks until the party."

Artemis sighed and rubbed her temples, lifting the arms of her glasses with her motion. "It shouldn't be this difficult to invite a man to his own son's birthday party."

"To be perfectly honest—" Luna stopped abruptly.

"Go on." Artemis raised an eyebrow at

her assistant.

Luna swallowed hard and looked at a spot just above Artemis's left ear. "He hasn't even met your son. Why bother reaching out at all?"

"Valid question." Artemis continued on the way to the secondary meeting room. "Trust me, I don't do it for me. If it was just me, I would never contact that bastard again. But Alexander may want to know his father. Maybe he's happy now, but in the future..." Artemis paused in front of a mirrored wall, checking her appearance for any flaws.

"You have a wisp of hair coming out of your French braid," Luna said, shifting her clipboard onto one hip and reaching into the bag swinging at her side. "I've got it, hang on..." She pulled out a comb and a travel-sized bottle of hairspray before working her magic to get the midnight-black hair to lay flat again. "And you've half chewed off your lipstick." Luna handed her boss a wipe to remove the rest while she searched in her bag for the small tubes. "Pink, nude, or red?"

Artemis studied herself in the mirror. Today, she was wearing a pencil skirt suit, high-waisted with a flared jacket. Underneath the jacket was her favorite sheer white blouse with small red cherries scattered across it. "Red, if it matches the cherries."

Luna popped the cap of the tube of lipstick and offered it to her boss, who swiped it over the back of her hand. "Perfect match," Luna decided.

Quickly applying the lipstick, Artemis blotted her lips, checked her teeth, and cleaned off her hand. "All good?"

"Couldn't be better," Luna said.

"There's no way I could do this without you. The amount of care I have to take in my appearance when a man can show up to a meeting with their shirt untucked and tie undone..." Artemis seethed for a minute.

"Did you catch a glimpse of Mister Mercury when he arrived?" Luna asked, surprised.

"I didn't need to. I know his type." Artemis rolled her shoulders back and continued on her way to the meeting room.

"He seemed pretty pissed when I instructed security to bring him here rather than your office." Luna trotted along beside her. She checked her clipboard. "And you have a board meeting in thirty minutes."

Artemis paused, one elegantly manicured hand resting on the handle of the door to the meeting room. She took the file regarding Mercury from Luna and opened the door. "No, I have a board meeting in ten minutes."

Ignoring Luna's gasp as the door closed between them, Artemis tapped the file into the palm of one hand as she examined the man who had come to meet with her.

Mercury was dressed exactly as she had predicted, shirt one size too large, untucked, with his tie loose around his neck. He hadn't even bothered to bring a jacket, as far as she could see. His hair was slicked back with so much product that she could smell it from across the room, although perhaps that was his cologne.

The guy didn't stand up to greet her, which...

Come on. Rude!

She tossed the file on the table between them and it slid toward him.

He put his hand on it, but didn't open it. "I hear you might be expanding your business."

Artemis raised a perfect eyebrow. "I have a few proposals I'm looking at," she said, not wanting to commit to anything. She hadn't looked at Charon's paperwork yet, afterall.

How does Mercury know about that?

"Is that really a wise idea?" Mercury sneered. "Maybe you should stick to what you know." He opened the file to reveal a blank paper. "What is this?"

"Your reason for being here," Artemis

quipped.

"There's nothing here."

"Precisely. Our meeting is done. Good day." She turned abruptly and left the room, leaving a spluttering Mercury behind.

Luna fell into step beside her. "You know, the last time someone talked to him like that, he sent them a deer's head in a box."

"I'm not afraid of him," Artemis scowled. "And if that's true, he should be *very* afraid of me."

"Yes, Miss Chase," Luna replied meekly.

"Submissiveness doesn't suit you, Luna," Artemis said. At the boardroom, she straightened her jacket, took the offered file, and raised her chin. "Bet?"

"Twenty mansplains, only three

correct."

"I'll take that." Artemis smiled. "Lunch on the loser?"

"ButterNut Bakery?"

"Where else?"

The meeting with the board members proceeded exactly as Luna predicted. The two women left the bank immediately following the closing remarks.

"Is there somewhere I can go to scream?" Artemis asked tightly. "I am so sick of being dismissed because of my gender!"

Luna nodded sympathetically. "Maybe you should join a gym or Odin's fight club, Valhalla's Throne, to blow off some steam."

That broke Artemis's bad mood. She burst into gales of laughter. "Can you imagine *me* in a fight club? I'd break a nail!" She got herself under control with difficulty. "No, I'll go to an extra pilates class. Do you think I can squeeze one in this afternoon?"

After consulting both Artemis's schedule and the local gym's classes, Luna said, "There's a class at two this afternoon that you can make if you can speed-read Charon's proposal beforehand."

"How many pages is it?"

"Three hundred."

Artemis gaped at her. "What?"

"Well, two hundred and ninety-eight, but I thought rounding up made more sense. It's single-sided, if that helps." Luna opened the door to ButterNut Bakery, and the tempting scents within washed over them.

"Not particularly." Artemis rubbed her temples as they got in line. "I need a break. No, scratch that, I need to get laid."

Luna chuckled. "That shouldn't be too difficult. I mean, look at you! You're gorgeous."

"Thank you for the compliment." Artemis sighed. "Unfortunately, guys look at me and are intimidated. It could be that I'm a Goddess, or maybe that I'm a CEO, or maybe just that I'm smart. Whatever it is, whenever I meet a guy, it doesn't usually end all that satisfactorily."

"Can I ask an impertinent question?" Luna asked hesitantly after she'd placed her order.

"You can get away with quite a bit. Go ahead." Artemis told Demi, the baker, her order, and paid for both lunches.

"How did you end up with Alexander's father?"

"He liked the feeling of power he got from being with me," Artemis said dryly. "Maybe I should amend my previous statement. It doesn't usually end satisfactorily for me *in bed*. The only good thing to come out of that relationship is Alexander."

"He's a darling," Luna agreed readily.

"Excuse me, I couldn't help but overhear," Hera, Demi's sister, said. "Artemis, you're looking for a guy?"

Artemis shrugged. "I'd settle for a good vibrator at this point."

Hera chuckled. "Tonight is Aphrodite and Eve's speed dating event for the month. Maybe you'll get lucky?"

"Speed dating?" Artemis said

thoughtfully. Then she shook her head dismissively. "It sounds like fun, but there's no way I could get a babysitter on such short notice."

"I could do it," Luna volunteered.

"I run you ragged enough during the day," Artemis protested.

"Then pay me double the going rate." Luna grinned. "I don't mind. I haven't seen Alexander in weeks."

"I met my mate thanks to them," Hera continued. "He's such a gentleman." She lowered her voice conspiratorially. "And I'm always more than satisfied."

"I..." Artemis blinked. "I guess I don't have a good reason to say no. Can you give me the details for the event?"

"I'll write it all down for you and bring them with your food," Hera told her. "Go find a seat."

"This is so outside my expectations," Artemis said, sitting at a table in the corner.

"Then maybe it'll work!" Luna said.

"Maybe." It looked like some of Luna's optimism was rubbing off on her.

Snag your copy of Artemis at your favorite online retailer.

Watch for the other books in the
Speed Dating with the Denizens of the
Underworld Series

Lucifer

Samael

Hecate

Demi

Hell's Belle

Hades

Orion

Cassiel

Hera

Triton

Alastor

Athena

Zeus

Medusa

Spike

Artemis

MEDUSA

Calliope

Mars

Pegasus

And More!

MORE FROM GINA

If you enjoyed this book, you may also enjoy…

Blackthorn Academy

Witch's Delight

Witch's Mystery

Witch's Pet

Witch's Baby

Speed Dating with the Denizens of the Underworld

Lucifer

Demi

Hera

Medusa

Artemis

FOLLOW GINA

Facebook
https://www.facebook.com/authorginakincade/

Newsletter Mailing List
https://landing.mailerlite.com/webforms/landing/r1r5n4

BookBub
https://www.bookbub.com/authors/gina-kincade

Blog/Webpage:
https://www.ginakincade.com/

Instagram
https://www.instagram.com/ginakincade/

Goodreads
https://www.goodreads.com/ginakincade

ABOUT GINA KINCADE

USA Today Bestselling Author Gina Kincade spends her days tapping away at a keyboard, through blood, sweat, and often many tears, crafting steamy paranormal romances filled with shifters and vampires, along with witchy urban fantasy tales in magical worlds she hopes her readers yearn to crawl into.

A busy mom of three, she loves healthy home cooking, gardening, warm beaches, fast cars, and horseback riding.

Ms. Kincade's life is full, time is never on her side, and she wouldn't change a moment of it!

Find more from Gina at:

https://www.ginakincade.com/

9 781773 575490